MOST GRIEVOUS
MURDER

MOST GRIEVOUS MURDER

Sara Woods

'A bloody deed, and desperately despatch'd!
How fain, like Pilate, would I wash my hands
Of this most grievous murder.'

Richard III, Act I, scene iv

St. Martin's Press
New York

Library of Congress Cataloging in Publication Data

Woods, Sara, pseud.
    Most grievous murder.

    I. Title.
PR6073.063M6   1982   823'.914   82-5779
ISBN 0-312-54908-3   AACR2

First published in Great Britain by Macmillan London Ltd.

First U.S. Edition

10 9 8 7 6 5 4 3 2 1

Thursday, 20th December, 1973

I

Meg Farrell leaned forward and asked earnestly, as though life and death might hang upon the answer, 'Why do you call it red tape, darling, when it's really a rather dreary kind of pink?'

'Really, Meg,' – Antony Maitland regarded her with a kind of exasperated affection – 'I haven't come three thousand miles or whatever it is to talk legal shop.'

'Three thousand, three hundred and forty statute miles,' said Roger Farrell helpfully, and exchanged a smile with Jenny Maitland, the fourth member of the party, who was sitting, listening quietly to the bickering, as she so often did. They were not above sharing a little gentle amusement, these two, over the vagaries of their respective spouses.

'But that's just what I'm complaining of, darling,' Meg protested, ignoring her husband. 'You're supposed to have come here to relax – that was the whole idea, wasn't it, Jenny? – and you're still obviously wrapped up like a cocoon in this stupid red tape of yours.'

'Give me time, Meg,' Antony pleaded, this time with a slight touch of apology in his tone. 'May I remind you that it's not much more than three hours since we landed, and though you and Roger have no doubt got used to the time change by now, for Jenny and me it's two o'clock in the morning, and this is our second dinner today.'

'I know, darling, you must both be worn out,' said Meg, looking with genuine sympathy at Jenny. 'But we've been rehearsing absolutely madly ever since we got here – at least, I mean, *I* have – so I haven't had time to notice whether I was tired or not.'

'You weren't,' said Roger bluntly. 'Otherwise' – he shared the confidence between the two Maitlands – 'she wouldn't have dragged me off to the opera every night.'

'Only twice,' Meg retorted. '*The Magic Flute* and *Simon Boccanegra*. And you know you loved them both, whatever you say now; and you know that I only get the chance to go out at night when we're rehearsing so I have to make the most of it.' She was better known to the theatre-going public as Margaret Hamilton, and had come to New York to help launch Jeremy Skelton's play, *Done in by Daggers*, which was still enjoying a successful run in London. Her permit allowed her two weeks for rehearsals and a month before an audience, after which, she would rejoin the original production at home in London. Roger, who was a stockbroker, and enjoyed his wife's popularity but sometimes resented – although he did his best to hide this – the evenings he had to spend alone, had elected to travel with her, leaving his clients at the mercy of his very able assistant, or if the worst came to the worst, the long distance telephone. They had travelled to New York the previous Saturday, and now Antony and Jenny Maitland had joined them, two days before the end of the Michaelmas term. Which gave Antony, a barrister, a slightly guilty feeling, even though he had managed to clear

6

his list completely before they set off.

'Anyway,' he said now, 'what's all this about my coming here to relax? If I'd wanted to do that I could have stayed at home and gone into the country.' He very rarely lost sight of a point that had been made, however the conversation might have strayed to different matters.

'It's just a manner of speaking, darling,' said Meg airily.

That was quite enough, as Roger could have told her, to confirm Maitland's suspicions. 'I'm beginning to suspect some kind of conspiracy,' he said. 'Are you in on it, Roger?'

'Not me.'

Roger was a man who could have posed any day for a portrait of a pirate, as he had done once for a young friend of the Maitlands, by instinct a man of action who had, at the same time, an incongruous streak of sensitivity to other people's feelings. Perhaps as a result of this, he was the only one of Maitland's friends to whom Antony was ever completely open.

'I think you said that a little too quickly,' said Antony consideringly. 'All the same I'll acquit you of any blame. When once we get into the hands of our womenfolk . . . Come on, Meg, out with it!'

It was Jenny who answered. 'As a matter of fact, in the first place I think it was Uncle Nick's idea,' she said. 'Or it may have been Vera's, I'm not sure about that. And Meg promised to try to help persuade you – '

'Which she did very effectively.'

' – and so did I, but only because I've been longing to come to America again ever since we were last here.'

'That's all very well, Jenny love, but why on earth should Uncle Nick think I needed a rest or whatever it was? And even more pertinently, why should he send me here to get it?'

7

'You know you're glad to be here,' cooed Meg.

'Of course I am, I can't imagine any better way of spending the Christmas vacation, particularly as you're both here too. But that isn't quite the point.'

'All right, darling, if you're going to cross-examine me I'll give you a straight answer,' said Meg, wrapping herself suddenly in a cloak of dignity.

'I wasn't exactly – '

'Weren't you?' Meg was a small woman who could assume equally well the role of gamine or grande dame. She had long dark hair, which she wore in a plait twisted round her head, except, of course, when the role she was playing on stage demanded another style. In fact, she had changed very little in all the years that Antony and Jenny had known her, except that she now dressed with such elegance and good taste that even the most observant person could rarely describe, after meeting her, what she had been wearing. 'Uncle Nick thought it might keep you out of mischief, being out of London for a while; and so may Vera have done for all I know.'

'Mischief?' spluttered Maitland. 'What does he think I am, still a schoolboy?'

'No, darling, but you must admit – '

Antony's eyes sought Jenny's. 'I once promised you,' he said, 'to stick strictly to my brief in future and never go beyond it.'

'And I told you to forget it.' Jenny's chin went up. 'You know perfectly well that you'd be – be less than yourself if you tried to keep your word about that. And this is just an idea that Uncle Nick and Vera have got into their heads.' (Sir Nicholas Harding was Antony's uncle and the head of the chambers in the Inner Temple to which he belonged, and Vera – previously Miss Vera Langhorne, barrister-at-law –

8

was his wife of two and a half years standing.) 'And I wouldn't have tried to persuade you to do anything I didn't know you'd enjoy,' Jenny added.

'All right, love, I understand now. It's this idea they've both got,' he went on, speaking directly to Roger now, 'that Chief Superintendent Briggs is running a sort of vendetta against me.'

'And don't you agree with them?' Roger asked.

'In a way, I do. You know that, I explained it to you once. But where we differ is that I can't see that it does any harm so long as I stick to the straight and narrow.'

'It nearly did a couple of months ago,' Jenny reminded him. 'A great deal of harm.'

'Yes, but those were exceptional circumstances. However,' he relaxed suddenly, 'I'm glad to be here so I won't grumble. How are the rehearsals going, Meg?'

He didn't get his answer immediately because they were interrupted by the business of ordering their meal, and being served the second round of drinks. 'I don't know what that pink stuff is you're drinking,' said Meg, watching the Maitlands' glasses being put down.

'Didn't you hear me order? Bacardi cocktails,' Antony told her.

'I'm sure this place has some proper sherry.'

'I'm sure so, too.' Antony paused for a moment to look around the dining-room, which verged on the palatial. 'But these things are very refreshing and after the journey ... for that matter, you've changed your aperitif too. I've never known you drink anything but Dubonnet.'

'When in Rome – ' said Meg vaguely. 'The martinis are terribly good here,' she added, assuming suddenly a mantle of sophistication, 'and Roger has learned the proper way to

9

ask for them, up with a twist. That means – '

'I know what it means,' Antony assured her, grinning, 'I learned the language when we were here before. But I was asking you, Meg, how the rehearsals are going?'

'Splendidly. I think Jeremy will be awfully pleased, and it's going to be as big a success here as in London.'

'They've got a good cast, then?'

'Absolutely splendid, and if you're wondering about the accents because the play's set in England, I took care of that,' said Meg proudly.

'How on earth do you mean?'

'Well, darling you know how it is. No Englishman can sound like an American, just as no American can sound like an Englishman, or only a very few in either case. So I got hold of the director – he's a little man very like Ossie and just as much of a dictator,' she put in in a sort of aside to Roger, 'and he rang Jeremy and explained my idea to him. So the play will be set in America, and there will be just a few lines added to explain the way I talk ... during the first month, that is, before Leila takes over.'

'Ingenious,' Antony approved. 'The Skeltons aren't here yet, then?'

'No, they're coming over for the opening and not before, because, of course, Jeremy's got another project on the way that's the most important thing in the world to him,' said Meg, smiling indulgently, 'and that's going to be the best thing he's ever written. But Anne,' she added, with a sudden reversal to her younger days, which they all gathered had been pretty frugal, 'has a far better grasp of essentials. After all, if they can get a reasonably long run here in addition to the London one, they'll be much better off financially.'

'I don't imagine they're feeling the strain too much even

without that,' said Antony a little dryly. 'Not that I don't wish them every success, I like them both.'

'And they like you,' said Jenny.

'Yes, I believe you're right, but you needn't sound so surprised about it.'

'I only meant that people often don't feel like that if they have a sense of obligation,' said Jenny carefully.

'Yes, well . . . never mind about that now. How do you like New York, Meg, so far as you've seen it?'

Meg wrinkled her nose. 'It's very dirty,' she said. 'It snowed the day after we got here, and you'd have thought it was the end of the world, but it didn't last.' Then she brightened. 'Of course, I love the Lincoln Center and this hotel is really very good. Our suite has a view over the park – '

'Central Park. So has our room,' said Antony. 'Though it's so enormous I think you might almost call it a suite too,' he added doubtfully.

'I keep forgetting you've been here before.'

'Not to the Hotel Majestic,' said Antony, smiling at Jenny.

'The place we stayed at last time was very comfortable too,' said Jenny. 'But, of course, we wanted to be with you, Meg, and I quite see you have to have something grander.'

'That's what I like best about New York,' said Roger suddenly. 'The chance of having my wife's company for part of the day, at least.'

'Now darling, you know you're enjoying yourself,' said Meg, answering the spirit rather than the letter of his words. 'There are lots of things to see.'

'Such as the view from our window over the park,' Roger suggested.

'Nonsense, darling, you know I didn't mean that. Anyway, it must be quite breathtaking when the trees are out,' Meg assured him. 'But what has really – has really touched me,' she assured Antony and Jenny, suddenly serious, 'is the way everyone at the theatre has accepted me.'

'They probably think it's an honour to be appearing with you,' said Jenny, quite as serious as her friend.

'Don't be silly,' said Meg, for once quite impatiently. Criticism she would have taken from Jenny like a lamb, but an implied compliment was another thing. 'Even Leila, the girl who is going to take over when I leave, doesn't seem to mind a bit that she's only understudying me for the first month. If we run as long as that, of course, I understand it doesn't always happen in New York.'

'It isn't quite like London,' Antony agreed. 'A bad review can damn a play, I understand.'

'Now that's funny, it doesn't seem to happen that way at home.'

'I can only suppose it's because our countrymen are more bloody-minded,' said Antony, 'and won't be guided by anyone else's opinion.'

'It isn't that at all,' said Jenny. 'Sam explained to me that it was all to do with bus trips from out of town, the people who run them daren't make the arrangements unless the reviews are good. And I understand what you mean about your understudy, Meg. Leila, did you say her name was? I've heard it said that the Americans are a generous people, but I think it's more than that. They're generous-minded.'

'Perhaps that's it, anyway it's a great relief to me,' said Meg. 'Of course, we've had a good deal of publicity about what happened on the first night in London, and quite a lot of people have asked me questions about that but I just told them that I wasn't on stage and didn't know anything about it.'

'Worth a guinea a box, I dare say,' said Roger lightly. 'The publicity, I mean. But here come our drinks. We'll see now how good you are at the language, Antony.'

II

By the time the Maitlands reached their room, the jet-lag was beginning to catch up with them. Antony sat down on one of the beds, too tired to undress immediately, and it was Jenny who noticed the little red-warning light near the telephone. 'That must have been a message,' she said. 'But who on earth could be calling us here?'

'I don't know,' said Antony, turning to look at the red light as though somehow it might prove informative, 'and I'm not at all sure that I want to know.'

'You mean, you think this publicity about the play is going to include our visit here,' said Jenny. 'Surely, nobody – '

'The press have their own way of finding things out,' Antony told her. He had pulled his tie askew, and was looking anything but professional. 'I was counsel for the defence, and the case caused quite a rumpus at the time.'

'All the same,' said Jenny, 'I think you'd better find out. It may not be them at all.'

'If you like.' He got up and walked around the bed he had been sitting on to the table where the telephone rested conveniently between the two. He was moving stiffly, as he so often did when he was tired and the pain in his shoulder a little nearer unbearable than usual. Jenny watched him anxiously, but made no comment. Sometimes she wondered whether she had been right all these years in carefully avoiding subjects to which some people would have said her husband was absurdly sensitive, but that was an agreement she

13

had made with herself years ago and it was too late to break it now. Jenny had a natural serenity about her that had many times stood her in good stead, so now she turned away as her husband reseated himself and picked up the receiver, and went across to the dressing table to brush her brown curls. All the same, she was alert to what was going on behind her.

'Operator?' she heard Antony say. And then, 'Maitland, Room 1104. I believe you have a message for me.' A pause, and then Antony's voice again, startled now, 'Sir Huntley? Oh well, yes of course. If you'll give me his number, I'll phone him in the morning. It's too late now.'

A longer pause this time. 'All right then,' said Antony. 'Of course I'll speak to him now if he made such a point of it.' He turned with his hand covering the mouthpiece. 'Nothing to worry about, love,' he said. 'Sir Huntley Gorsford, I can only think Uncle Nick must have told him we're here.'

'It's getting awfully late, Antony,' Jenny pointed out, twisting round to face him.

'Yes, I know, you heard what I said to the operator, but she told me Sir Huntley had insisted that I call him however late it was when I got to my room. And, of course,' he glanced at his watch, 'it won't seem quite so late to him as it does to us.'

'I suppose we should be flattered,' said Jenny doubtfully. 'The Ambassador himself.' She broke off as her husband raised a finger to silence her, removed his hand from the mouthpiece, and turned his attention to the telephone again. 'Thank you, operator,' she heard him say, and then, 'Sir Huntley?' It seems rather late to be returning your call, I hope I got the message correctly, Your Excellency.'

The voice that replied to him was undoubtedly that of his uncle's old friend, whom he had known since his boyhood, though latterly Sir Huntley's activities had kept him out of

14

England for most of the year. 'Not so much of the "your excellency",' he said now, though beneath the apparent joviality Antony thought he could detect a thread of uneasiness. 'You didn't call me that during the early years of our acquaintance.'

'That's a long time ago,' said Maitland with truth. 'Besides, you weren't Her Majesty's Ambassador to the United States of America then.'

'True, true. But I think we'll dispense with the ceremony, if you don't mind. I've a favour to ask you.'

'Of me?' The cautious note was back in Maitland's voice again. Then, recollecting himself, he added vaguely, 'Anything I can do, of course.'

'Wait till you've heard me out,' Gorsford warned him. 'And that won't be tonight, it's too long a story and you only flew in today. I can imagine you're wishing me to the devil already.'

'Well,' said Antony, suddenly amused, and hoping that the amusement was reflected in his voice and correctly interpreted.

'I know, I know. It's goodness knows how long since you saw your bed, I'm really sorry about that, Antony, and I hope you'll apologise to that pretty little wife of yours.'

This time Antony's smile was sternly suppressed. If Jenny had been six foot two with a figure in proportion instead of a very trim five foot seven, Sir Huntley would have referred to her in exactly the same way. 'I'll do that,' he promised. 'And about this story of yours which is too long to tell me now?'

'Too long and too private for the telephone,' said Gorsford, suddenly brisk. 'Do you think you can drag yourself from your bed by lunchtime tomorrow?'

'If I know anything about it, I'll be awake at two o'clock your time, or three at the latest,' Antony assured him. 'Though I can't say,' he added frankly, 'that I shall be over-keen on getting out of bed at that time.'

'No need, no need. What I was going to suggest was that you get on a train down to Washington. Amtrak, that is. You'll find a seat's been booked in your name. They'll give you a decent lunch, it only takes three hours, and is much more restful than coming down on the shuttle. I'll have a car to meet you, you must stay at the Embassy overnight, and we can have our talk in peace.'

'But – '

'Jenny won't mind being left alone for one night,' said Sir Huntley, so briskly that Antony was more than ever convinced that he had only just remembered the name. 'These friends of yours – '

'Yes, she'll be all right, but how did you know we were here?'

'The press, my boy, is in many ways a wonderful institution.'

'Damn the press,' said Antony with feeling.

'No doubt you often feel like doing so, but it has its uses at times. Can I rely on you, Antony, will you catch that train?'

'I can't think – '

'You know what Nicholas would say, never theorise ahead of your data,' said Sir Huntley, and now he sounded smug. 'It's an important matter, as you must have surmised by now, and I think you're the person who can deal with it better than anyone else.'

'I'm not a diplomat,' Antony pointed out.

'No, you're not, are you?' If there was a sting in the tail of that remark, it was rapidly glossed over. 'You're a man with

16

a flair and a knowledge of foreign languages that borders on the miraculous – '

'I've forgotten everything I ever knew,' said Antony hurriedly.

'Then the sooner you remember again the better, although I think only French and German are involved. However, since we seem to be in agreement – '

'I didn't say I'd come.'

'But you will,' Sir Huntley asserted. 'And unless I'm much mistaken you'll come with Jenny's blessing.' He concluded by giving Antony briskly the time of the train and the station from which it left and rang off before there could be any further argument.

Jenny was listening unashamedly now. 'What on earth was all that about?' she demanded.

Antony told her. 'I don't seem to have much choice but to accept,' he concluded gloomily.

'Well, I'd much rather you were here, but I couldn't bear it if you didn't find out what it's all about,' said Jenny frankly. 'Roger and I can go sight-seeing while Meg is rehearsing, and perhaps we'll go to the theatre in the evening; but anyway I'll have their company, and you'll be back on Saturday.'

'All right then. I'm like you ... I'd probably never sleep easy again unless I find out what the old boy wants. But it does seem peculiar. I mean, all I know is the law, and that can't be what's the matter. All his staff has diplomatic immunity, and even if they hadn't I couldn't help them here.'

'That's what makes it so fascinating,' Jenny assured him. 'But you'd better get to bed, Antony, or you'll be fit for nothing tomorrow. I know I'm worn out.'

Whatever might be said to Sir Huntley Gorsford's detriment
– and like most people with a few ideas of his own, he wasn't
universally popular – it had to be admitted that when he
made an arrangement it went like clockwork. Maitland
followed his instructions to the letter, and found himself at the
Embassy in Washington by mid-afternoon, being greeted by
profuse apologies for the fact that Sir Huntley was engaged,
offered a drink he didn't want, and being allowed finally to
compromise with tea. The tedium of waiting was enlivened
by one of Sir Huntley's aides, a young man who caused
Antony a good deal of amusement by seeming to be con-
tinually on the verge of what he obviously felt would have
amounted to an indiscretion ... that of admitting that,
though he wasn't aware of Antony's present errand, he knew
him perfectly well by reputation, and was therefore inordinately curious.

Sir Huntley bustled in at last, preceded by another and
even larger china teapot. He was a tallish man and might,
thought Maitland, eyeing him as they greeted each other,
have posed at any time for the portrait of a typical English
diplomat. His hair was grey and still plentiful, his moustache
rather darker and neatly trimmed to prevent a tendency to

bristle, he had a ruddy complexion and rather bright blue eyes that always seemed to be open to their widest extent. For the rest, he was perfectly turned out, in a way that made Maitland, with his preference for the casual, regret that the clothes he normally wore in the course of his profession were at home in London. He had a dinner jacket with him for Meg's opening night and any other occasions that might arise to require it, but even to visit Her Majesty's representative in the United States he could hardly wear it during the day.

'Always have a cup at this time of day,' Gorsford announced, and finally he seated himself and Antony was able to follow suit. 'Pour Mr Maitland another cup, Tim. Nonsense, of course you haven't had enough, can't stand those fiddling little cups myself.' Antony passed his cup meekly, and watched with some dismay while a quantity of very dark liquid was poured for His Excellency into what looked very much like a pint pot. 'Sugar? Milk?' asked Sir Huntley, helping himself copiously to both and looked disapproving when Antony refused either embellishment. 'The only way to neutralise the tannin,' he said. 'All right, Tim; that's all, we'll help ourselves.' (Not if I know it, Antony thought.) 'But don't let anybody – anybody at all – disturb us for a couple of hours.' Tim disappeared, amusing Antony again because he would have sworn he never saw the door open or shut, but suddenly the young man was gone.

'Well, now,' said His Excellency, coming immediately to business and eyeing his companion severely, 'what I have to tell you is in the strictest confidence.'

'That's understood. But – '

'There are no buts about it. You're ready to listen, wouldn't be here if you weren't,' said Sir Huntley, reminding

Maitland for a moment of his Aunt Vera who also had an elliptical way of speaking, though to a far more marked degree. 'Got an assignment for you.'

'I gathered that – '

'You're on holiday, I know that.' Sir Huntley interrupted him again. 'Far too many holidays, that's the trouble with you legal chaps. And this is important.'

'I've no experience in diplomacy.'

'Of course, you have, taking the word in its widest sense,' said Sir Huntley, apparently forgetting his strictures of the evening before. 'You don't blunder in just anyhow when you're examining a witness, do you? But, in any case, that's not what I want you for. Heard this and that about you over the years. Good at summing up people, aren't you?'

'I imagine as much can be said of you, sir, and of every one of your staff.'

'Not in the way I mean.' He paused, glaring into space, and then turned abruptly to face Antony again. 'Better be plain,' he admonished himself.

'Yes, that might be the best thing.'

'And no laughing at your elders and betters either. I told you this is serious.'

'I wouldn't dream of it, sir.'

Actually no two men could have been more unlike in appearance than Sir Huntley Gorsford, K.C.B., and Antony's uncle, Sir Nicholas Harding, Q.C. Nevertheless, at this point Maitland began to notice certain resemblances between them. So he sustained a long, hard look from the Ambassador with comparative calm, put down his cup with the unpleasantly strong brew no more than sipped, and settled himself in his chair, assuming what he hoped would be recognised as a receptive attitude.

'Have you heard what happened in New York a week ago?' asked Sir Huntley abruptly.

'A lot of things, I imagine.'

'You must have read about this, it was all over the papers.'

'I've been rather preoccupied, trying to get things cleared up before we came away. I don't remember anything in particular.'

'No interest in world affairs, you young people,' grumbled His Excellency. Maitland, who hardly felt that this description fitted him or that the accusation was fair, assumed all the same a look of penitence. 'Peter Ngala, the Ambassador from Timkounou to the United Nations, was murdered right outside the building,' Sir Huntley went on impressively.

'Outside the United Nations building?'

'What did you think I meant?'

'How did it happen?' asked Maitland, ignoring what was obviously a rhetorical question.

'He was gunned down by rifle fire, an automatic rifle they presume, from a car that had been parked down the road and started up as soon as he appeared.'

'And that was bad?'

'Of course it was bad!' said Sir Huntley, obviously refraining with difficulty from adding the words, 'you fool!'

'I don't even know where Timkounou is, I'm afraid.'

'In Africa.'

'Yes, I did know that much,' said Antony dryly. 'But all these new names – '

'Can't blame you, I suppose. The dead man was the son of the President of Timkounou, Joseph Ngala, who happens to be an old friend of mine.'

'And you want to see justice done,' said Maitland, as though light had suddenly dawned on him. 'I'm sorry, sir, but the police are much better equipped for dealing with that kind of thing.'

'Justice is all very well,' said Sir Huntley, rather grumpily, 'but it's an international incident I'm trying to avoid. It's exactly the same with your uncle,' he went on in a complaining tone. 'Nicholas will never let you get a word in edgeways.'

'I'm sorry,' said Antony, rather taken aback by this sudden attack. 'Of course I'll listen to whatever you have to say.'

'That's better! Perhaps I should start by telling you about my long association with Joseph Ngala. I was at Oxford with him ... Magdalen. I think we drifted together because our fathers had been friends too, still were at that time, of course, both of them still alive. My father served as District Officer in Timkounou in colonial days, it had a different name then, of course, but I won't burden your brain with that, and it happened that he had helped Joseph's father out in a legal matter regarding tribal rights and territory, for which the old boy was inordinately grateful. Well, Peter and I became pretty close friends – '

'Yes, Your Excellency, I can see that makes matters difficult for you, but after all it isn't as if the murder took place on British soil.'

'I told you before, no formality,' growled Sir Huntley. 'What I'm trying to tell you, if you would clear your mind of all these pre-conceived notions of yours, is that I know Joseph Ngala pretty well.'

'I see,' said Antony rather blankly.

'You will in a minute,' the Ambassador promised. 'And rid your mind, once and for all, of the vision of Joseph mourning for an only son. Peter was one of seventy-nine, or something like that. Not that they weren't on good terms, and he was the eldest, that makes a difference, you know.'

23

'Yes, I can imagine it might.'

'Laughing at me again,' grumbled Sir Huntley. 'I'm just going to get back to the murder and I'd have thought that was right up your alley.'

'In a manner of speaking, yes,' said Maitland cautiously.

'I told you Peter was cut down outside the United Nations building, at about four o'clock on Friday afternoon, just a week ago. There were lots of people around, of course. You won't have had time to notice it yet, but Americans start celebrating around Thanksgiving and go on until Christmas is over, and all that time the traffic's heavy and the streets are crowded with pedestrians. So there was no lack of witnesses.'

'All telling a different story, I suppose,' said Antony gloomily.

'Yes, that surprised me a bit. I should have thought two people viewing the same incident would each have been able to describe what happened fairly well.'

'It never has happened that way, and I dare say it never will,' said Antony.

'You ought to know. The only thing the police did get some agreement about was the car, and one man even claimed to have seen the number plate and to have made a note of the number. If he was right, that made the ownership easy to trace, and the number was found to belong to a car belonging to Tengrala Nema, who is the son of the Bosegwane Ambassador to the United Nations.'

'Oh no!' said Maitland faintly.

'What's worrying you? The unfamiliar names, or the plethora of ambassadors?'

'Both, I'm afraid.'

'It gets worse rather than better,' said Sir Huntley sympathetically. 'So the police went to see young Nema – '

24

'Could they do that? Diplomatic immunity and all that,' Antony added vaguely.

'As it happens this Tengrala doesn't qualify. He's on bad terms with his father, the Ambassador, in this country without his permission, and there's no connection at all with the Embassy. You know that there's a school of thought that holds that in criminal matters diplomatic status can't be claimed, and that can lead to endless wrangling, but in this case the position seems quite clear. In any event, if the matter were referred to Louga – '

'To whom?'

'Louga Nema, the Ambassador, Tengrala's father. What I'm saying is that it would be quite open to him to waive immunity for any member of his suite, and in the case of his son there's no doubt that he would.'

'I'm sorry, sir, you were telling me that the police questioned this young man – '

'Yes, and he said he had no idea that his was the car used, but it was quite likely because it had been stolen from outside the block of apartments where he lives a couple of days before. And sure enough, the following day – I mean the day after the murder – a filling station operator over in Brooklyn reported it as having been abandoned on his premises some time during the previous night. There was nothing to show definitely that it was the murder vehicle, only some rather suspicious-looking scratches on the door at the passenger's side, which could have been interpreted as having been made when the window was wound down and a weapon rested there until the instant came to fire it. It was an almost new car so that was rather difficult to explain, and Tengrala insisted the paintwork had been in perfect condition the last time he saw it. In any event, the long and the short of it was, the police applied for a search warrant and had a look round young Nema's apartment.'

'You're going to tell me they found the murder weapon there.'

'They did, but that wasn't all. The place was bristling with automatic rifles, well just one room really that was used as a sort of store-room. Cases and cases of the things.'

'That must have given the police fun, trying them all out until they found the right one,' Maitland commented. 'So what did they do then?'

'It was a tricky situation, as you can imagine,' said Sir Huntley, 'even with the young man's complete independence from his country's delegation. I mentioned a certain amount of behind-the-scenes activity going on, the State Department and all that. But I don't think there's any doubt it will end up with a warrant.'

'How many people were in the car?'

'There's a fair amount of unanimity among the witnesses about that, as a matter of fact. There was the driver, and there was the man who fired the shots.'

'Fingerprints?'

'Someone had taken the trouble to go over the interior of the car pretty thoroughly, and the door handles too. As for the rifle, that was as clean as a new pin.'

'This – what did you call him? – Tengrala Nema wouldn't have needed to take his own prints off the car.'

'That might quite easily be construed as a double bluff.'

'And you really think he'll be arrested?'

'Yes, I do.'

'But I don't see why that should worry you so. You might well be concerned with Peter Ngala's fate, as he's the son of an old friend of yours. But this Tengrala – '

'There are wheels within wheels,' said His Excellency por-
tentously. 'Perhaps you don't realise the political situation
between Timkounou and Bosegwane.'

'I didn't know there was one. They're both in Africa, but
I haven't the faintest knowledge of them other than that.'

'Then I must explain. They're adjoining states, Bosegwane
the more southerly of the two. Timkounou, as I have told you,
is headed by a President, my old friend Joseph Ngala, and it's
one country where I think I may say that the withdrawal of
colonial rule has met with a fair amount of success. Joseph is
what you might call an enlightened ruler.'

'I still don't see.' Maitland's tone was becoming very faintly mutinous.

'Bosegwane, on the other hand, can only be called back-
ward in comparison with its neighbour. It is ruled by one
Mbongo, who declared himself King and rules now in a des-
potic fashion. But – '

'I have a feeling,' said Antony, when His Excellency
paused impressively, 'that you're about to come to the heart
of the matter.'

'Indeed, I am. There are, in Bosegwane, large deposits of
uranium. Added to this, there is a long history of provocative
incidents against Timkounou, border scuffles, things like
that, which Joseph tells me – and I believe him – are invari-
ably instigated by the Bosegwanians. Now, I know Joseph,
Antony, and I know there's nothing he would like better than
an excuse to invade Bosegwane, overthrow "King" Mbongo,
and take over the government himself. He would certainly
use the country's natural wealth more wisely,' he added
thoughtfully.

'You're going to tell me that the murder of his son gives him
a very cogent reason for such an invasion. What I don't see

is why that would be such a bad thing, as Ngala is – what did you call it, sir? – enlightened, and this Mbongo apparently isn't.'

'If we were operating in a vacuum,' said Sir Huntley rather aggressively, 'Her Majesty's government would like nothing better than that things should fall out as you have just described. However, there are other matters to consider. The Russians have long regarded Bosegwane as, to some degree, a protégé of theirs. They, in turn, would be happy to take any strife of the kind you have outlined as an excuse to intervene. Not in person, I hope you understand at least so much of foreign affairs, but through one of their surrogates.'

'I think,' said Antony slowly, 'I'm beginning to see where you're heading, Your Excellency, and I'm quite sure I don't like it.'

'If Tengrala Nema is proved to have killed Joseph Ngala's son, Joseph will order his troops to move on Bosegwane, you can be sure of that. He'll give as his reason that the murder was committed at the instigation of the Embassy. But if the world could be convinced to the contrary, he has sufficient regard for public opinion to hold his hand. Now, Antony, there have been occasions when you have been able to help on occasions of this kind – '

Maitland got up and began to stride angrily about the big room. It occurred to him later that this probably constituted some frightful breach of etiquette, but if so Sir Huntley remained unmoved. 'You're not thinking of me as a sort of one man department of dirty tricks, by any chance?' Antony demanded.

Sir Huntley's round-eyed look was the very personification of innocence. 'Why ever should I do that?' he wondered.

'You've already mentioned my reputation at least once.'

28

'And where was the harm in that?'

'If you're thinking I'll fake evidence to prove that this Tengrala is innocent,' said Antony, 'I tell you straight, I won't do it!'

'I think, you know,' said His Excellency meditatively, 'that when we speak of reputations, you and I must be thinking of something entirely different. Tell me your version, if it isn't too much of a bore.'

'Oh, I've heard the stories. The man who never loses a case,' said Maitland bitterly.

'And don't you?' asked Sir Huntley ingenuously.

'Of course I do, you know better than that, sir. But I've been accused of being unorthodox – which is probably true – and things have got into the papers sometimes, and the police – '

'Will it help if I assure you that my request to you was perfectly above board, and has the blessing of Her Majesty's government? Now, wait a minute,' he raised his hand as Antony was about to break into impulsive speech again, 'it's going back a good many years but you may remember an occasion when you were of the greatest service to the Intelligence Department. That hasn't been overlooked in official circles, I can assure you.'

Antony came to a halt and stood looking down at his companion. 'That was one of the episodes that has led the police – certain members of the force, that is – to regard me with some suspicion ever since.'

'I'm sorry about that.' But the regret was perfunctory, Sir Huntley was intent on making his point. 'If young Nema is guilty, he'll have to take his chances,' he said earnestly. 'But that's by no means certain. I don't think you should condemn him unheard.'

'You want me to see him?'

'That, at least. And if you then find it reasonable to extend your inquiry – '

'That's all very well, sir, but what about the Americans? They'll hardly take kindly to my poking about on their territory. Meddling, Uncle Nick always calls it.'

'I've no doubt he does.' Sir Huntley's smile was reminiscent. 'However, there have been discussions at the State Department – '

'I'm not really accustomed to quite so rarefied an atmosphere, sir.'

His Excellency ignored this. 'I don't think,' he said thoughtfully, 'that the – the possibilities of the situation are quite so well appreciated there as they are in Westminster. But they'd be glad enough to be rid of an embarrassing situation, the son of the Ambassador, even though he's here unofficially ... I needn't elaborate, need I?'

'You mean they won't take offence at my activities. What about the police?'

Sir Huntley smiled suddenly. 'We must just trust your discretion, that's all.'

'And if I talk to this Tengrala Nema and decide he's guilty?'

'You'll still have earned my gratitude.'

'Nothing else will be expected of me?'

'Not a thing. But by what I've heard of you, I very much doubt whether you'd be willing to play judge and jury to quite that extent.'

'You're right about that, of course,' said Maitland rather ruefully. 'There's just one thing that makes me feel I might accede to your request.'

'You'd be doing your country a service – '

'If things turn out as you wish.'

' – and maybe the whole world, as well.'

'Come now, sir, that's putting it a bit strongly, isn't it?'

'You only say that because you don't understand how subtle the difference between war and peace can be.'

Antony thought that out for a moment. 'You may be right,' he agreed, but rather doubtfully. 'What I was going to say was that there's one thing that strikes me about this story of yours. Why the devil should Tengrala Nema have killed the Timkounou Ambassador anyway?'

'I can think of no motive at all.'

'Still there are all these rifles. What did he want with them? Like you, sir, I can think of no motive, unless he wanted to provoke the very war you're afraid of, which might go some way to explaining the cache of weapons.'

'Still, you'll see him,' said Sir Huntley.

'I haven't said so yet. For one thing, I'm not looking for trouble, but I think you should grant me diplomatic status for the duration of the enquiry.'

'No difficulty about that, my boy.'

'I haven't quite finished. I suppose now you're going to stress the delicacy of the mission, and emphasize the need for absolute secrecy. I tell you plainly, sir, it won't wash.'

'Why not?'

'Jenny and I are here on holiday, she'll be expecting my company most of the time. And this – forgive me – is such a bizarre request that it will need some explaining.'

'I've met Jenny,' said Gorsford, 'and I've always understood from Nicholas that the pair of you could discuss the most confidential matters in front of her. I think there can be no objection – '

'That's not quite all, sir. There are the friends we're with.'

'From what I read in the paper ... an actress and her husband,' said Sir Huntley doubtfully.

'*The* actress, some people say,' Antony corrected him. 'And contrary to anything you may have heard about that profession, Meg has a hatred of gossip that is almost pathological. And as for Roger ... if this wild goose of yours leads me anywhere, I may need his help. So the diplomatic status I referred to should apply to him too.'

'Do you feel you can trust him?'

'I've done so many times. And you know, Your Excellency, it may not be tactful to mention this, but I'm inclined to regard my own professional activities rather more seriously than I do this assignment of yours.' He paused there, and perhaps he was conducting some sort of examination of conscience for he added reluctantly after a moment, 'for the time being at any rate.'

'Then that's good enough for me.' Sir Huntley came to his feet as he spoke. 'On your own terms, Antony, and you have my very best wishes for your success.'

'I shall need them,' said Maitland with feeling. 'But there may be nothing I can do, you know.'

'I realise that. Well, we've been talking long enough. Come and meet some of the other members of my staff, and you'll find we can offer you something a little stronger than tea.'

Antony was grinning as he followed His Excellency out of the room. Anything stronger than the cup of tea he had just left half finished would, he thought, put him under the table in double quick time.

Saturday, 22nd December

The rest of the visit passed pleasantly enough, though Maitland, not unnaturally, was eager to get back to New York. The
subject of his talk with Sir Huntley wasn't mentioned again,
except once when he was briefly alone with the Ambassador
just before he left. 'You do understand, sir, that I've only
agreed to try to see Tengrala Nema. He may well refuse to talk
to me, but if he agrees, what I do or don't do afterwards will
depend on the impressions I get during the interview.'

'I thought you lawyers were trained not to make judgments
before all the evidence was in.'

'But this chap won't be a client,' Antony protested. 'That
makes a difference, you know. Anyway,' he added, and
couldn't keep a certain hopeful note out of his voice, 'the odds
are he'll be completely surrounded by lawyers, who won't let
me anywhere near him.'

Sir Huntley laughed, probably because the other man's
feelings were so very transparent. 'I have great faith in your
ingenuity,' he asserted, and no more was said on the subject,
though Antony couldn't help feeling, as he thought matters
over on the journey, that he wished he shared the older man's
confidence even to some small extent.

He had some trouble in finding a cab at Penn Station

33

and it was nearly four o'clock when he arrived back at the hotel. Jenny wasn't in their room, but he guessed, rightly as it turned out, that she would be with Roger and Meg. The only question was whether they were in or out, but the day being unpleasant, it was probably more likely that they would be indoors. A phone call to the Farrells suite confirmed this, and as soon as he had washed off some of the grime of the journey he made his way there. Roger let him in. 'Come into the sitting-room,' he invited. 'It's absolutely enormous, much larger than ours at home, and pretty comfortable on the whole. I've just ordered tea.'

Pausing for a moment on the threshold – it was indeed a very large room – Antony thought with amusement that even if he hadn't already known it, he would have guessed immediately that Roger was one of the occupants. Jenny always said he reminded her of the man who couldn't go into a room without ejaculating 'Boom' which startled ladies greatly, and though this wasn't precisely accurate, it was certainly true that his arrival never went unnoticed, and that there generally occurred in his surroundings a certain subtle disarrangement – drawers and cupboards left open, books and newspapers left lying about everywhere – that made his presence quite obvious to the discerning eyes of his friends.

'Come in, darling, we can't wait to hear what it's all about,' Meg invited. 'Or is it something too frightfully hush-hush? I shall probably die of curiosity if it is.'

Jenny had appropriated a corner of the sofa and curled up there much as she did at home. It was immediately obvious to her that her husband was tired, he was moving stiffly as he did when his shoulder was more painful than usual, but it was against her principles to refer to this in any but the most oblique fashion. 'Whatever Sir Huntley wanted you for,' she

34

asserted, 'it's something you don't like.'

'You're quite right, love. I don't like it at all,' Antony agreed. He crossed the room, pausing to give Meg a brotherly peck on the cheek as he went, and stooped to kiss Jenny before he flung himself down on the sofa beside her. 'And as for its being confidential, Meg, it is . . . very. I have Sir Huntley's permission to talk to you about it, however.' He paused, considering, and then smiled. 'I suppose I blackmailed him into that really. But it isn't the sort of thing we ought to discuss in the bar, for instance.'

'We're private enough here,' said Meg hopefully.

'So we are. As soon as the tea arrives and the waiter's gone again, I'll tell you,' he promised.

Meg's eyes widened. 'He hasn't asked you to murder somebody, has he?' she said.

'On the contrary. But you'll really have to wait, Meg.' Fortunately, at that moment the tea arrived. Jenny eyed the small metal pots doubtfully but removed the tea bag from Antony's and began to pour without comment.

'There's nobody in the bedroom, or the bathroom, or in any of the closets,' said Roger when he had passed the cups. 'So you may as well satisfy Meg's curiosity, Antony.'

'And yours, darling,' said Meg. 'Don't tell me you're not dying to hear what it's all about.'

'It's a complicated story,' said Antony, but launched into it without further hesitation.

When he had finished, 'That's all very well,' Roger objected, 'and you say you may not take the matter any further than an interview with this chap who apparently makes a hobby of collecting weapons. But how are you going to get to see him?'

'I shall call on him – we shall call on him, Roger, did you

35

gather I meant to involve you in all this? And if he won't see us, that's the end of it.'

'But what reason?'

'That's fairly simple. Bosegwane is a member of the Commonwealth, Her Majesty's government is concerned about the fate of one of its subjects. Not a word, of course, about the reasons for their concern.'

'I see. And if he's retained a lawyer or lawyers?'

'The same story would have to serve for them. If we can put it over tactfully, it oughtn't to upset them too much.'

'And the police?'

'Would that they may never hear of me,' said Antony lightly. 'But there again – '

'They'll think you're interfering,' said Roger bluntly.

'And they'll be quite right. If I take the matter any further, that is. It isn't my idea and I don't like it any more than you do,' he added, looking around so that the remark was shared between all three of his companions, 'and I don't mind telling you I'd have refused outright if it hadn't been for the deeper implications.'

'And if this chap really did murder the Timkounou Ambassador to the U.N.?'

'Matters must take their course. There's nothing you or I or anyone else can do about it, if Joseph Ngala is determined on war, as Sir Huntley thinks he is.' He picked up his cup, the tea was almost cold now and he drank it thirstily, and then went on anxiously, 'Was I right in thinking you'd help me, Roger?'

'I've never known you to need any help when it came to asking questions.'

'No. What I want is moral support. And perhaps a witness.'

'Do you have to ask? You know I'll come with you. But we

do have a few engagements over Christmas.'

'The conversation with Tengrala Nema needn't interfere with those,' Antony told him. 'In the meantime, supposing we want to, we can get quite a bit done. Are you rehearsing tomorrow, Meg?'

'Neither today nor tomorrow,' said Meg luxuriously. 'Jenny and I will be perfectly all right, and I shall only be at the theatre for a short time on Christmas Eve.'

'By then, I may have decided to chuck the whole business,' said Maitland. 'What do you say, love?'

'You must do what needs to be done, of course,' said Jenny, as he had known she would. 'You needn't worry about me, there are a thousand things to do here, and if I don't feel like doing any of them alone, I can always go down Fifth Avenue and look at the shops. The only thing is . . . do you think this man you're going to see still has all those automatic rifles?'

Antony smiled at her. 'Jenny, love, of course he hasn't. The police took them away to see if one of them killed Peter Ngala . . . remember?'

'Yes, but they might have given them back again, and just kept the one that did.'

'Put that right out of your head. They certainly wouldn't hand them back. So you can forget all about the possibility of his shooting either Roger or myself.'

'If you say so,' said Jenny doubtfully, 'but I don't think he sounds quite a nice young man.'

'Bless you, love, I don't suppose he is. Though come to think of it, I've no reason to say that.'

'It isn't the act of a nice young man to keep a hoard of automatic rifles in his flat,' Meg pointed out in her most dignified manner. Then she grinned. 'But I quite agree with you, darling, the police have drawn his claws and so long as

37

you and Roger are together, there's nothing for either Jenny or me to be alarmed about. Only you won't forget the party at the theatre after the opening, will you?'

'I'm looking forward to it,' said Maitland, not altogether truthfully, and exchanged a glance with Roger. 'But I hope this business will be settled long before then. And there'll be no doing anything on Christmas Day, even if I decide to continue, so the arrangements we made, the dinner here and all the rest of it, still stand.'

'That's good,' said Meg with satisfaction. 'Personally I think it's all a nonsense and won't detain you for more than a day or two. And I think you ought to remember, darling, that if the Russians want to intervene in Africa, they'll intervene, with or without an excuse. I don't think this Sir Huntley of yours has thought it out properly.'

Once more Antony and Roger exchanged a glance, this time as much exasperated as amused on Maitland's part. 'I dare say you're right, Meg,' he said pacifically. 'In any case, there's no use arguing about it. Who lives may learn.'

By mutual consent, the subject was avoided for the rest of the evening, only when they were getting ready for bed did Jenny refer to it again. 'I don't know how you remember all these people's names,' she said, and Antony had no doubt to whom she was referring. 'But this one who had all the rifles, he sounds like a terrorist to me. I don't know that Uncle Nick would think it an awfully good idea for you to get mixed up with him.'

'Jenny love, I'm only going to try to help him,' Antony pointed out. 'Terrorist or not, I don't see how he can take exception to that.' Jenny was silent then, but he realised from the look on her face that his argument had come nowhere near convincing her.

38

Sunday, 23rd December

I

After lunch the following day Jenny and Meg set out for The Cloisters, about which Meg had been reading in a guide book, leaving their husbands rather pointedly to their own devices. 'All right,' said Antony, getting up rather reluctantly, 'let's try our luck. If our quarry isn't in or refuses to see us, we can always follow them on their excursion.'

Roger came to his feet with rather more alacrity. 'What exactly is my part in all this?' he inquired, but not as though the answer particularly concerned him. 'I've always thought I'd make quite a good bodyguard.'

Maitland looked at him for a long moment. 'So that's occurred to you too?' he said, making the words a question.

'What do you mean?'

'Jenny said Tengrala sounded like a terrorist type. I don't think I succeeded in reassuring her,' he added rather ruefully, 'but I'm as certain as I can be of anything that if that assessment is correct the last thing he'd do is attempt any mayhem in his own quarters. Particularly in the circumstances. I shall introduce you as a colleague, if we get that far, that is. And if anything occurs to you to ask him, for heaven's sake come

39

out with it. But what I really want is a witness.'

'I thought your activities had the approval of the authorities.'

'In a way. But I don't suppose there is any more liaison between the State Department and the New York police than there is between what Sir Huntley rather stuffily called Her Majesty's Government and Scotland Yard. There can't be any real trouble, but it may not be possible to avoid a certain amount of unpleasantness.'

'I hadn't thought of that,' Roger admitted. 'Very well then, let's get on with it.' He made purposefully for the door of the room.

Outside the hotel there was no trouble in picking up a cab, and the journey across town to the east side address that Antony had been given didn't take long through the Sunday traffic. Paying off the cab they found themselves looking up at a tall building, obviously not in its first youth but with certain pretentions to elegance, and rather dwarfed by the taller buildings on either side. 'Convenient,' said Antony tersely, and added, in response to Roger's inquiring look, 'Only a step to the United Nations Building.'

Here the Sunday afternoon quietude was even more marked. It was, as Antony had rather feared, one of those buildings where you press the buzzer beside the name of the person you want to see, and thereafter – if he chances to be in – have to explain yourself into a sort of grating on the wall. Having done that, you may or may not be admitted. However, there was no help for it. He found the name NEMA, and pressed the button beside it, and after what seemed an interminable interval a voice out of nowhere said 'Please?' inquiringly.

'Mr Nema?'

'Tengrala Nema. Who is it please?'

40

Antony introduced himself and added the explanation he had already rehearsed. 'I have a colleague with me, a Mr Farrell,' he went on.

'Not from the police.'

'A colleague,' Antony repeated patiently.

There was a silence. 'I will let you in,' said the voice at last. 'Come in quickly when the buzzer sounds. Some of my friends do not move fast enough.' But Roger was already gripping the door handle, and they had no difficulty in entering the inner lobby.

When the lift stopped at the third floor a young black was waiting for them on the landing. 'I am Tengrala Nema,' he said with a hint of pride – or was it defiance? – in his voice. 'You are the gentlemen who wish to see me?' He was darker than Maitland had expected, and also younger, probably not more than twenty-three or four. 'A good looking lad with pretty manners,' Roger was to describe him later to Meg and Jenny, but at that moment he was as nervous as a cat.

Antony introduced himself and his companion again, but there had been enough of explanation, he thought. Meanwhile, Tengrala was eyeing them both closely, but then he appeared to make up his mind and turned abruptly on his heel.

'Come,' he said.

They followed him down a well-carpeted corridor until he stopped outside a door marked 303. Here they had to wait a moment while he produced a key and let them in. 'You will understand,' he said, 'I do not wish to be surprised.' And then, turning and smiling with a flash of very white teeth, he added rather ironically, 'It is good, but also rather surprising, that the British Government takes so much interest in my affairs.'

'Have you employed a lawyer, Mr Nema?'

'But certainly I have. I see, Mr Maitland, you know a good deal about my affairs. But sit down, gentlemen,' he added without waiting for a reply, 'and then you can tell me how I may serve you.'

'The question is,' said Antony seriously, 'whether we can be of help to you.' He selected a chair and waited until the others were seated before he went on. 'I do know something of your affairs, Mr Nema, but not as much as I should like.'

'You know about the shooting. Do you too think I am a murderer?' he asked challengingly.

'I have to admit,' said Maitland, 'that I have no opinion at all on the subject. I know that the police have visited you – '

'Several times.'

' – and that the weapon was found in your possession. But now you have a lawyer to advise you, and he is conversant with the laws in this country as I am not – '

'I will tell you something about this lawyer,' said Tengrala. 'He is a nice man, black like me, and perhaps he is as wise as I have been told. But he will not believe me when I tell him that I had nothing to do with this affair.'

At this point Roger seemed about to say something, and Antony spoke quickly before he could do so. 'Before we go any further, Mr Nema, I must make the position quite clear to you. Any communication you make to your lawyer is privileged . . . do you understand what I mean?'

'Perfectly well.'

'I too am a lawyer, but with no standing in this country. If you talk to me, no such privilege will exist.'

Again there was the hint of irony. 'I thought all lawyers were men of discretion.'

42

Antony smiled. 'There can be no question of withholding information where our ambassador is concerned, but I'm not trying to say that your confidences would be broadcast,' he assured him. 'Only that, if the police take the matter further and it comes to trial – ' He didn't attempt to complete the sentence and after a moment Tengrala spoke slowly.

'I understand, of course. One thing this lawyer has told me, and that is that if it were not an embarrassment to the United States government I should have been arrested already. Do you think that is true?'

'Very likely.'

'They asked me – oh, very politely – for my passport.'

'Did they though? Well, as I told you I don't yet know all the circumstances.'

'And for some reason you would like to. Perhaps for the one you have told me, perhaps for another reason that is more subtle,' said Tengrala and sounded pleased with the word. 'Perhaps you will tell me, at least, how it will be of help to me if I talk to you.'

This time Roger had his say. 'Mr Maitland is not without experience in these matters. If you're innocent, it can do no harm to confide in him, and perhaps may do you some good.'

'And if I am guilty?'

'Are you?' asked Roger bluntly. This time Maitland, having delivered his warning, did not intervene.

'No, I am not. But I ask again, what could your friend do for me?'

'If you're telling us the truth, he might be able to find the guilty party,' said Roger, and here Antony found it advisable to intervene again.

'Mr Farrell is exaggerating,' he said. 'I would certainly try to do so, but that is a very different thing from succeeding.'

43

'Try then!'

'I don't think you understand, Mr Nema. If I do make such an attempt, it can only be done through you.'

'I have no interest in Timkounou. Why should I have murdered Peter Ngala?'

'The relationship between your two countries has not been uniformly peaceful.'

'That is nothing to me. "King" Mbongo, as he calls himself, does not consult me as to his actions.' There was a world of scorn in his tone.

'He's the head of your country – '

'And therefore I should be loyal to him?' For the first time something like anger sounded in Tengrala Nema's voice. 'He calls himself King, which is foolish, and under his rule our country makes no progress. My father is his man and because of the way I feel he has disowned me. I tell you, he will do nothing to help me in this matter.'

'I'm very sorry to hear that. But I say to you again, Mr Nema, that the assassin of Peter Ngala can only be found through you.'

'Tell me what you mean.'

'Because the automatic rifle with which he was killed was found in this apartment. Along with others, and for your own sake I think that should be explained too. If it were only that your car was used that might have been fortuitous, but the rifle could only have been taken by someone known to you, and who knew of its presence here.'

'Do you not think I have thought of that? That I haven't realized that I can trust nobody, not even my closest friends?'

'Yes, I'm sure that must have occurred to you.'

'But now perhaps, you can help me.' For a moment he sounded almost as though he were talking to himself. 'I wish you would call me Tengrala,' he said. 'When you say, Mr Nema, I think of my father, and this is something I do not wish to do.'

'Very well, Tengrala. Does that mean you're willing to talk to me?'

'You have been honest with me, Mr Maitland, in explaining your position in this.' (Antony had a mental grimace for that, but comforted himself with the reflection that what he had said was the truth, if not the whole truth.) 'I think I will trust you in return. But I must tell you before anything else that I have no idea who took the rifle and returned it.'

'That's a pity, but we can narrow down the field a little. I take it, as the police are so suspicious of you, that you can't produce an alibi for the time in question.'

'Friday, December 14th,' said Tengrala. 'I was here all the afternoon. And if I had wanted to do such a thing, which would have been madness, I had no car.'

'Let's deal with that first then. Where was the car kept?'

'This building is too old to have its own arrangements, but there is a parking garage across the street. I rent space there by the month. But when it was taken it was parked in the street.'

'With the keys left in it?'

'No. But I understand there are ways – '

'Never mind that for the moment. It was stolen three days before the murder? That would be the eleventh of December? Did you inform the police?'

'Not then.'

'I think you must elaborate on that a little, Mr ... Tengrala. Why did you not inform them?'

'I thought perhaps that one of my friends had borrowed it for some purpose.'

45

'Without telling you?'

'It might have been a sudden emergency.'

'A very familiar friend then.'

'I suppose you could say so. I don't know many people in America, Mr Maitland, but I suppose you could say that those I do know, I know intimately.'

'Did you ask your friends?'

'None of them had taken it.'

'Or enquire if it had been returned to the garage?'

'Why should the thief have done that. Besides, they might have insisted on the police being informed.'

'When did you tell them then ... the police I mean?'

'The first time they came to interview me. That was fairly soon after the assassination, because one man on the scene had apparently noticed the number plate. The car wasn't found until later, a couple of days later, I think.'

'So you told them what had happened, I presume they made some enquiries themselves.'

'Yes, but they didn't tell me anything about that.'

'I see. What about the car keys?'

'There are two sets. One which I carry on me, the other which is kept in the top drawer of the bureau over there. I couldn't find them when I found out the car was gone, that was one reason I was pretty sure that one of my friends had taken both. But the police asked me to look again ... and there they were!'

'That raises another question, but let it go for the moment. How long have you been in the United States, Tengrala?'

'About nine months. And in this apartment, which is furnished, since a few days after I arrived.'

Antony paused to look around him, until now his attention had been focused on the object of his questioning. It was an utterly impersonal place, none of the ordinary signs of occupation that people impose on their surroundings. 'And you came here without your father's consent?' he said.

'I think you should put it a little more strongly than that. He was actively against my coming.'

'Why was that?'

'I told you he had disowned me.'

'In that case, what you do should be of no further concern to him.'

'You are talking like a white man.'

'I don't quite understand you, Tengrala.'

'He would feel shame at any of my doings that did not fall in with his wishes.'

Maitland frowned over that information for a moment. 'The position is,' he said at length, 'that you were here alone on the afternoon of the 14th, that you could not, in any case, have taken part in the assassination because your car had been stolen several days before though you did not report that fact to the authorities. In your defence, you will say that you had no motive for murdering the head of the Timkounou delegation to the United Nations, but if I were advising you as your lawyer I would tell you that your story of being at odds with your father might have repercussions you didn't foresee.'

'I don't quite understand you,'

'You didn't like the government in your own country. It could be said that the murder of Peter Ngala was a deliberate act to provoke his father into taking action against Bosegwane.'

'There is no truth in that.' There could be no doubt that he was genuinely indignant at the idea. 'Timkounou is nothing to me.'

47

'Well, you have explained to me, after a fashion, why you didn't inform the police of the loss of your car. How do you explain the cache of rifles found somewhere in this flat? I know you are under no obligation to justify yourself to me,' he added, seeing a spark of anger in the young man's eye, 'but you offered to trust me, after all.'

'And so I do.'

'Well then, what were the rifles doing here?'

'I have an interest in such things and am a collector in a small way.'

'How many weapons?'

'Three dozen.'

'One of which killed Peter Ngala. Tell me, were they all different examples of their kind?'

'No.'

'All the same model?'

'Yes, they were,'

'I don't know how a court would receive that story, Tengrala, for myself, I find it quite incredible.'

'You do not think I would be believed?'

'Not a hope of it.'

'We are speaking in confidence?'

'Subject to the reservations I explained to you, yes, we are. And I am speaking for my friend, Mr Farrell, too.'

'Very well then, I shall tell you, and you will see that it is not a story I can use in my defence.' Again there was a flash of very white teeth. 'I came here to buy arms, no other reason, and to recruit some friends who will help me. It is our intention to overthrow this foolish "King" of ours, who, in addition to being a fool, is also a despot, and replace him with a president with more enlightened ideas.'

'Yourself for instance?'

'I am not yet old enough. There is a man we follow, but I do not think I will tell you his name.'

'And all this is to be accomplished with thirty-six automatic rifles? I admit they're deadly weapons, but – '

'Nothing of the sort. There is already a considerable armoury – do you call it? – well hidden in Bosegwane.'

'That raises the question, how did they get there?'

'That was not difficult. Each country, you know, has its own diplomatic bag. By degrees – '

'You're telling me you're plotting with the Timkounou delegation?'

'No, no, no. I have friends in Cauguera who are willing to be of assistance.'

'What's in it for them?' asked Maitland rather crudely.

'When the new regime takes over power there will be trade agreements, you know my country is rich in minerals, particularly in uranium. But, of course, this is a circumstance which should not get about.'

'It sounds like a ruddy mess to me,' said Maitland frankly. 'Is it because your father knows what is going on that he objects to your presence here?'

'No, he knows nothing about it. He thinks of me only as a playboy ... I think that is your word for one who lives only for pleasure, without a thought in his head. And perhaps up to two or three years ago he would have been right about that. Now I am very careful that he should not know how my ideas have changed.'

'Changed so much that you would contemplate overthrowing an unpopular regime by force?' Tengrala nodded emphatically. 'Tell me something. If Peter Ngala had, in some way, stood in your path, would you have removed him?'

The dark eyes opened very wide as though in wonderment,

so that, incongruously, Antony was reminded for a moment of Sir Huntley. 'But of course,' said Tengrala simply.

'Murder?'

'When one is engaged in an activity for the good of one's country one cannot afford to consider these – these bourgeois concepts.'

Antony took time to think of Jenny's strictures. 'That is something I think you should keep to yourself,' he said. 'Over here it is a point of view that would hardly be appreciated.'

'An American would not hesitate to take such action,' said Tengrala positively.

'You've been seeing too many gangster movies,' Maitland told him. 'I should have said it wouldn't be appreciated by the ordinary law-abiding citizen. And that brings us to these friends of yours, one of whom I must suppose has, or had, a key to this flat. Or rather, two keys, one to the downstairs door as well.'

'In New York, it is called an apartment,' Tengrala corrected him, which in Maitland's opinion was no more than a device to gain time before answering.

'Never mind that! Someone got in and took the car keys from your desk and later returned them. Someone took a rifle, used it and returned it too. Unless you're in the habit of leaving your door open, that someone had the means of entry.'

As he had done before Tengrala said vehemently, 'Do you not think this is something I have thought about and thought about. I am not in the habit of leaving my door open, I never have been, and only one person had the keys.'

'As far as I'm concerned, that should simplify matters.'

'Nothing of the sort. You are saying, are you not, that somebody tried deliberately to have me blamed? Margaret

50

could not possibly have had anything to do with that.'

'Margaret?'

'Margaret Charron. She is an American girl, but you must believe me, Mr Maitland – '

'How many friends have you who have visited you here?'

'Six in all.'

'Including this Miss Charron?'

'She prefers to be called Ms. And yes, I was including her.'

'And are all these people known to each other?'

'Very well known.'

'Co-conspirators of yours?' Maitland insisted.

'I suppose you might call it that. I would rather say people who are interested in human rights and in justice.'

'Tell me about them,' said Antony simply.

'What is there to tell?'

'You might begin with their names, and then go on to their occupations. But, wait a minute, how are you living here yourself? I mean, if your father no longer supports you . . . do you have a job?'

'That would interfere too much with what must be done. I have funds at my disposal . . . from the party at home that I support,' he added rather grandly.

'I see. About these friends of yours then.'

'I told you you needn't consider Margaret.'

'But I may have to find out from her who could have obtained the keys you say she has. So I think you should tell me a little about her, if you don't mind. About her family, for instance.'

'I don't know anything about them except that she comes from California and I believe her father is well-off by standards over here. She seems rather ashamed of that. And she says she's been in New York for three years, but she left home

51

long before that.'

'How does she live?'

'It's none of my business. I only know that she has all the right ideas, a proper understanding of the way things are and the way they ought to be.'

'Her ideas parallel yours.' Perhaps Maitland should not be blamed if his tone was a trifle sardonic.

'That's why we're friends.'

'And she has keys to this flat – this apartment? Is she living here?'

'No. And if you think that is because I'm black, you are wrong. It is because she already has this thing going with another American, a man called Joel Harte. She knows I'll be going back to Bosegwane before too long, so she doesn't want to fall out with him.'

'You mean he's supporting her?'

'Yes. He had this apartment in the Village – Greenwich Village – but quite a fancy place, so she just moved in with him a year or so ago, I believe. I'd be willing to help her out – out of the fund, you know – but I don't think he's the man to stand for that, he'd wonder how she'd made the money. And he has a good job in one of the big Trust Companies down Wall Street way.'

'Is he too a friend of yours?'

'Why not, man? He is a very enlightened sort of fellow.'

'Does this enlightenment include sharing your views of acts of terrorism?'

'That's what *you* call them, Mr Maitland. I say we're at war and that makes a difference. And you won't call it terrorism when we take over the country. I know your language very well, that will be a *coup*.'

'*Touché*.' Antony smiled at him. 'But I gather from your

remarks that this Mr Harte is not prepared to throw up his well-paid job and take part himself in the actual liberation of Bosegwane.'

'Just a sympathiser,' Tengrala agreed.

'Is he in your confidence?'

'Margaret told him.'

'She was taking a chance, wasn't she? Who knows how he might have taken it.'

'She has some principles.'

'You'll forgive me, I thought you were describing a purely mercenary relationship.'

'She wouldn't take a penny of his if he didn't think the right way about things.'

'I see. I should apologise to her, I suppose. But you mentioned six friends . . . associates . . . in all. What about the rest of them? Are they all men?'

'Three of them are. There is one other woman, Noella Crashaw, she's American too, and I don't know even as much about her family as I do about Margaret's, but I should say she's about the same age. She shares lodgings with the other three men, and I think she's as much in sympathy with their ideas as Margaret is with mine. And when I say share, I mean exactly that. She lives with one of them, Jean le Bovier – '

'I knew there was a Frenchman in it somewhere,' said Maitland triumphantly. 'Is he the one who introduced you to the phrase bourgeois concepts?'

'Yes, I suppose so. He is a former member of the French Foreign Legion, and so are the other two men.'

'Are they also French?'

'No, one is Irish and the other German. Michael O'Shaughnessy and Friedrich Schiller.'

'And how do they live?'

'I told you I have funds. It won't be long now before we're ready to move.'

':Mercenaries in fact?'

'Aren't *you*, Mr Maitland, when you accept a client and he pays his fee? That needn't interfere with your wanting justice to be done.'

'I suppose you're right about that,' said Maitland rather startled. 'Do you have any other information about these three men?'

'No, when I came over, I was told to get in touch with them. They introduced me to Margaret.'

'And they all knew about the arms that were being smuggled out of the country?'

'They all knew.'

'Including Joel Harte?'

'Oh yes, certainly.'

'And they have all been here many times?'

'All our meetings were held here. To tell you the truth, I'm sure they found it more comfortable than their own place.'

'Yes, I can understand that. So we have to consider, Tengrala, whether any of them could have obtained the car keys without your noticing – '

'I don't think that would have been very difficult. It was no secret where they were kept.'

'But hardly the kind of thing to come up in casual conversation. However, we then come to a more difficult point . . . the rifle. Could that have been removed and later replaced without the use of these keys Miss Charron holds?'

The young man scowled over the question. 'You're trying to involve her,' he declared.

'Certainly not. I asked you a simple question, and I should very much like an answer. Or perhaps you can tell me that

54

your own keys were once out of your possession long enough for another set to be cut.'

'If I told you that, it wouldn't be true. And the rifle couldn't possibly have been taken while I was in the apartment. Or returned either.'

'Then we've got to find out what happened to those keys. Perhaps you can help us there, Tengrala. When did she last use them?'

'She hasn't been here alone since the police first questioned me about the murder. I would think it was the afternoon of the thirteenth.'

'The day before Peter Ngala was killed?'

'Yes, somebody could have done what you say might have been done with mine, have borrowed the keys and had another set cut.' He was suddenly eager again. 'Don't you see, Mr Maitland, that could be anybody?'

'I'm afraid not, Tengrala. Somebody who knew the rifles were here, and that, according to what you've told me, brings it down to the six people you've named.'

'Now I see,' said Tengrala despondently. 'But,' he added, brightening, 'the same thing applies to them as applies to me. What motive could they have for killing Peter Ngala?'

'That is something that must be determined. If you had to guess – '

'That's something I don't want to do. They are comrades, don't you understand, Mr Maitland?'

'Yes, I understand and in a way I sympathise. But remember that whoever it was, was quite willing to make it appear that you had committed this crime.'

'Well, I suppose ... Joel would have had the most opportunity of getting Margaret's keys, and he is not perhaps quite so committed to our cause as the others.'

'Yes, that's a very valid point. There is something else I think you can help me with, though. I know very little of the political situation in your part of the world.'

'Things are as they have always been,' said Tengrala. Antony and Roger exchanged a glance, after all he was very young. 'At home there is anarchy, the poor go hungry and have no hope. This is what we would change.'

'How would your party propose to set about that?'

Tengrala looked at him almost pityingly. 'We are a rich country,' he said. 'That is, we can be if we use our resources properly. It has been promised,' (Antony had the impression that he had almost spoken his leader's name), 'that money will be spent to relieve the people's misery. This is what I wish to fight for.'

'Even against your own father?'

'What else can I do? He is old and set in his ways. While the "King" he supports is ruler there will be no change.'

'And with whom will you trade?'

'In raw materials with the West. This is not ideological, you understand,' (again Antony had the impression that this was a word heard from one of his recent companions), 'they can supply us with the things we need, for farming, for industry, and then in other small matters we will trade with our neighbours.'

'Your neighbours are Timkounou and Cauguera?' said Antony. He turned to Roger. 'I looked at H.E.'s atlas,' he said. 'Bosegwane is a small country completely encircled by its two larger neighbours, so that they also have a common border.'

'In the interior, in the hilly country,' Tengrala amplified. 'They are at peace because it is too difficult to keep troops in that region.'

'Perhaps they don't want to fight each other,' Maitland

56

hazarded.

'Perhaps not.' Tengrala shrugged. 'Cauguera is, in any case, a poor country without our resources, which is why trade agreements with us would be valuable to them. Don't you see, Mr Maitland,' he was suddenly earnest, 'in benefiting our own people, we should also benefit theirs.'

'But your own relations with Timkounou have not always been so peaceful?'

'No.'

'Whose fault is that?'

'It is the fault of jealousy, and one of the bad things that "King" Mbongo does. But they are not unwilling to carry the fighting back over our borders when it suits them.'

'Which is why you weren't surprised when I implied that their president, Joseph Ngala, might make it a pretext to invade your country if you were proved to have murdered his son.'

'I think he would like such a pretext, but he values world opinion too and does not wish to become an outcast.'

'How would *you* regard such an action, Tengrala? Might it not bring about the very state of affairs you desire?'

'And live under the rule of Timkounou? Never!'

'Then you will see that your predicament may have consequences even beyond the obvious ones which may be very unpleasant to yourself.'

'Yes, I understand it now you have explained it to me.'

'And you still maintain that the six people that you have mentioned are the only ones to know of your cache of weapons? That nobody else may have visited here and stumbled upon it accidentally?'

'They have been my only visitors, my closest associates. I told you, I do not know many people in America.'

'No members of the Embassy to the United Nations, your own countrymen?'

'Them least of all. They would be too afraid of my father to make any friendly overtures to me.'

'Then you will agree – won't you? – that one of your six friends, at least, must be implicated in the murder? If only as the supplier of the car and the rifle.'

'My head tells me this must be so, but my heart will not agree to it.'

'Then I must ask you, Tengrala, do you wish for my help?'

'Do you wish to help me?' the young man countered.

'Yes, very much.'

'But you were here as a judge, were you not? I thought . . . many times I thought you did not believe me.'

Antony smiled at him. 'If you mean that I was sometimes sharp with you, Tengrala, my friends would tell you that I should have been much more polite if I hadn't been half way, at least, to believing your story. Do you want me to be quite honest? I disapprove of many of your ideas, and on the question of a revolution in your country I am not qualified to judge. I want to believe you when you say you didn't kill Peter Ngala, and I am almost sure I do, but I know myself well enough to realise this may be wishful thinking. Do you still wish me to try to prove that somebody else was the assassin? As I pointed out to you before, I have none of the obligations towards you that a lawyer would have to a client. Therefore, if I come to believe in your guilt, I shall drop the whole thing like a hot potato.'

Funnily enough, the first thing that seemed to strike Tengrala Nema about this statement was the way it was worded. 'That is a strange phrase,' he said thoughtfully, 'but very expressive. I think I have no alternative but to accept

58

your help on your terms, it seems I need it very badly.'

'Will you give me the addresses of your friends?'

'I will write them down for you.' A small sigh accompanied this promise but he got up without hesitation and went across to the desk. Before long, he came back and handed Maitland a sheet of paper. 'I have not been to either of these places,' he said. 'As I told you, my friends have visited me here.'

'I may want to see you again,' Antony warned him.

'That will be my pleasure. Unless, of course, in the meantime the police . . .'

'What is the name of the policeman in charge of the case?'

'Lieutenant Hennessey.' That was perhaps the most difficult name he had had to pronounce so far.

'I suppose you don't know which precinct he belongs to.'

'No. It may have been on the badge that he showed me, but I didn't notice.'

'I expect that will be quite easy to find out. And the name of your lawyer? May I go to see him?'

'If you wish, his name is Adams. I think perhaps his office will be closed until after the holiday, but there should be no difficulty about that. He lives in this building.'

'I see. Before we go, may I suggest that you see him again yourself and are perfectly frank with him, both as to the extra set of keys and the reason for the rifles being here.'

'I will think about it.'

'Think hard,' Maitland advised. 'I must thank you for your patience, Tengrala. Whatever happens, I shall do my best to be in touch.'

II

The lobby was deserted when they got out of the elevator, and half way across Maitland stopped dead and turned to his companion. 'It may be not altogether wise, Roger,' he said, 'but I have a strong feeling we ought to talk to this Mr Adams before we do anything else.'

Roger looked all round him before replying, but every door was tight shut. 'Can it do any good?' he wondered.

'I shouldn't think so.' Antony sounded almost cheerful. 'A matter of professional etiquette,' he added vaguely.

Roger, who after all knew him very well, wasn't deceived for a moment by the vagueness. 'You're not acting in this affair in any way in a professional capacity,' he pointed out.

'That's true, but all the same ... will you come with me?'

'I can see you've made up your mind, and of course I will. But there's one thing I should like to know, Antony. Are you taking everything that young hooligan said at face value?'

Maitland considered. 'Yes, I think so,' he said. 'He's not stupid, you know.'

'I never said he was.'

'Then think about it for a moment. If you were in his situation, couldn't you somehow have thought of a better story than the one he gave us to account for the rifles, for instance?'

'I think they'd be pretty hard to explain.'

'Yes, of course, but think about it,' said Antony again. 'He admitted he saw nothing wrong in terrorist tactics if the situation, as he saw it, seemed to justify them. That was hardly calculated to arouse our sympathy, was it? But, so far, he doesn't seem to have indulged in any tricks like that.'

'So he says.'

'So he says and I think I believe him. And this proposed revolution, I don't think *that* story would make him exactly popular with the American authorities, do you?'

'There's gun-running going on all the time.'

'That doesn't mean it's approved of.'

'I don't see what they could do about it, though, since the embassy of this other country – what did he call it, Cauguera? – seems to be involved.'

'They could declare him *persona non grata* and pack him off out of the country.'

'Better than being tried for murder.'

'You know, Roger, I somehow don't think it'll come to that. That's partly why I want to talk to Mr Adams, he's the one with the expertise in these matters over here after all.'

Roger, who seemed to regard the proposed interview with misgivings, raised a further objection. 'For one thing, it appears he doesn't believe your friend Tengrala,' he said. 'For another, you're going to have to go outside again to look up the number of his flat, and then explain yourself to him over that damn telephone.'

'No need. You can hold the door open while I look at the list of tenants ... or didn't you think of that?'

'Of course, I did. I don't think it's a good idea to take him completely by surprise though.'

'That's what we're going to do, however, if he's in.' A moment later he was back with the information. 'He's here on the ground floor,' he said. 'Number 101. Come on, Roger, let's try our luck.'

As visitors had normally to announce themselves by telephone, there was a knocker on the door, but no bell push. Maitland tapped lightly, and then after a moment, a little more insistently. After a further interval, the door was opened by a stout black lady in a brightly coloured, very well-cut dress. She showed no surprise at the sight of two unannounced intruders but smiled at them warmly and asked, 'Can I help you?'

'Are you Mrs Adams?'

'Yes, I am.'

'It's your husband we want to see, if you think he won't regard it as an intrusion to call on him at his home about a purely professional matter.'

She didn't answer that directly. 'You're British,' she said in a pleased way as though the discovery delighted her.

'Connected with the Embassy in Washington,' Maitland told her. 'They're concerned about a member of the Commonwealth, a fellow tenant of yours, in fact – '

'That boy, Tengrala!' she exclaimed, half exasperated.

'Tengrala Nema, yes. You know him then?'

'Naturally. We're Americans, you understand, but I think he was glad to find someone here of his own colour.'

'I'm sure he was. Will you ask Mr Adams – ?'

'He will be glad to see you, I'm sure of that. Meanwhile,' she beamed at them again, 'I will be making some tea. That is what you British like at this time of day, isn't it?'

'Very much,' said Antony sincerely. 'We'll try not to keep your husband very long,' he added.

'He will not mind. He is only reading the *Times*,' she added. 'If we are not doing anything on Sunday, that usually takes him the whole day. He will be glad of a rest.'

A moment later Maitland was introducing himself and Roger to the lawyer, and explaining his errand all over again, and just as guardedly. They found Mr Adams to be just as stout and friendly as his wife. 'No need for apologies,' he said. 'If it is an intrusion it is a very welcome one. I share your concern for this young man, Tengrala, whom Hetty and I have become very fond of, but I fear there is no doubt that he has done this dreadful thing.'

'We have just been talking to him, my colleague and I, ('as if anyone could get a word in edgeways with you present,' said Roger later) 'and he denies very strongly that he was responsible for the murder of Peter Ngala.'

'And he gave you, also, his explanation that he is a collector of automatic rifles. Quite frankly, Mr Maitland, did you believe him?'

'No, I didn't.' Which was true enough.

'And even if this very unlikely story were to be believed, one of those rifles was the murder weapon, no doubt about it. That must be explained, and the use of his car must be explained, and if that had really been missing for several days as Tengrala maintains, why had he not reported its loss?'

'Those things are true, but there is also the question of the motive.'

'Who knows? I fear my native country is not altogether a happy place these days.' He saw Maitland's inquiring look. 'No, I have no idea which part of Africa my forebears came from,' he said, 'and if I had,' he added smiling, 'I'm sure the name would have been changed since then.'

'I thought each country was going back to its original name,' said Roger.

'That is true. Perhaps, after all, my ancestors would recognise their homeland. As I said, there are many rivalries, many jealousies. Who knows what may have motivated this very foolish young man?'

'You think that is how an American jury would view the matter?'

'We haven't got as far as that yet, Mr Maitland.'

'I should be grateful if you would explain to me what you feel

63

Tengrala Nema's position is as far as the law is concerned.'

'I think the authorities are in something of a dilemma. On the one hand, they are in no doubt of my client's guilt, on the other, there is the embarrassment of dealing with a foreign national, a man so nearly connected with his country's embassy to the United Nations, although he himself has no diplomatic status.'

'Then which way do you think the cat will jump?'

'I think the matter will be decided eventually by public opinion. There has been much grumbling, as I am sure you can imagine, about the abuse of diplomatic privilege.'

'There is also a good deal of precedent for disregarding diplomatic status in criminal matters.'

'You sound very much like a lawyer yourself, Mr Maitland,'

'Yes, I'm a barrister. Which is why the Ambassador, who has known me since I was a boy, felt I might be the best person to discover the exact position. You feel that public opinion may be sufficient to make the police proceed as far as an arrest and trial then?'

'I think it is a distinct possibility.'

'Have you talked with Tengrala's father?'

'Oh, yes, I made it my business to see Louga Nema very soon after his son consulted me. I feel there is no possibility of his intervening on Tengrala's behalf, though if you wish to try your powers of persuasion on him, Mr Maitland, please believe I should have no objection.'

'You are very kind, and kinder still to take me on trust in this way. I have no intention of interfering professionally, but I don't think I need assure you of that. My interest in the matter is purely diplomatic.'

'So I have been assuming,' said Mr Adams in his deep

voice. 'In any case, we have talked only of things that all the world knows. I understand your Ambassador's concerns, Mr Maitland, but you can assure him that everything that can be done for Tengrala, will be done.' As he spoke, the door opened and Mrs Adams entered with a tea tray.

There was a handsome silver service, and the tea itself, as Antony had feared, was strong and rather bitter. But he was so enchanted with his hostess that this hardly occurred to him until later, and he accepted the cup that was offered to him without even a mental grimace.

'And have you finished your professional business?' she asked him with a smile.

'Indeed we have, madam, and the tea will be most refreshing,' said Antony sitting back and preparing to enjoy himself. But at this moment, Roger made one of his rare incursions into the conversation.

'Mrs Adams,' he said, 'it has occurred to me that perhaps you are very often at home during the week when your husband is about his professional duties.'

'During the week and very often at other times,' she assured him, still smiling. She glanced at her husband before she continued. 'Crime may occur at any time, and a trial lawyer is not altogether master of his own working hours.'

'That's what I thought,' said Roger with satisfaction. In his turn, he glanced at his friend. Maitland was smiling but showed no inclination to take over the questioning. 'You've been so kind to us, Mr Adams,' Roger went on, 'I hope you won't consider that we're going too far if we ask your wife a few questions.'

'If she has no objection to answering them, neither have I.'

'What are these questions then?' Mrs Adams sounded intrigued.

65

'You know Tengrala Nema quite well. I wondered whether he had confided in you in any way.'

'If it was a confidence, I might not feel able to repeat it. But there is no need to worry, he spoke of his home sometimes, of his disagreement with his father and how his mother felt about that. Nothing that could interest either of you.'

'His friends here, did he ever mention them?'

'No, never, but I will tell you one thing. He had a mistress.'

'That is the first I've heard of that, Hetty,' said Mr Adams mildly.

'Because it is none of our business, Edward. I knew you would not approve any more than I do, but it is the way of young people today and we older ones must live with it.'

Maitland put down his teacup and was now sitting forward in his chair. 'The girl was living with him, Mrs Adams?' he asked.

'No, not that, but a regular visitor. I met her several times in the hall, often enough that we would greet each other. Always in the afternoon. And one day as we were passing, she dropped the keys she held. I stooped to pick them up, thinking nothing of it, but couldn't help noticing that one was the key to one of these apartments, they're rather a distinctive shape, and the number 303 was only too clearly visible. I admit I was surprised, she was a beautiful young woman, very fair, but there could be no other reason for her having a key to Tengrala's apartment and visiting him so often.'

'I see.' Maitland had taken over again, and Roger was only too glad to leave him to it. 'Was this fair young woman the only one of his guests you ever saw?'

'No, there were three men who came together and rang our bell. This was soon after Tengrala had moved into this building. I don't think they knew him at that time, they had

66

obviously mistaken the name, but when we had talked for a little they told me it was a young black man they were seeking, and I was able to send them up. Afterwards, I encountered them several times in the hall.'

'Are you able to describe these three men?'

'After all this time – ' she said doubtfully.

'I know it's difficult. But at least you can tell us, were they as young as Tengrala is?'

'Oh no, that at least I can tell you. I am not good at ages, and – if you will forgive me – especially of white men. But I would say in their late thirties, perhaps. And I can tell you their nationalities,' she added, 'because, though they all spoke to me in English, their accents were very different from yours, or from ours for that matter. It was a Frenchman who did most of the talking, a little, very tidy man. And one of the others, who also talked a good deal, I think was Irish. A big man, not fat, with a cheerfulness that was missing in the other two. The third man hardly spoke at all and so I can't be sure, but my impression was that he was German. All I remember about him is that he had too much hair, which is not the sort of impression you get of men of his race from the war films. But everything changes as we know.'

'Mrs Adams, that's a marvellous effort of memory, and I'm truly grateful to you. You say you saw these men again, presumably visiting your young friend?'

'Yes, I saw them all at one time or another, but not all at once again. Sometimes the little Frenchman was with a girl, I can't remember what was said but I heard her speak to him once and she was quite definitely an American. A little dark girl, even smaller than her escort. I think, perhaps that would appeal to him.'

67

'You're quite right.' Antony smiled at her. 'We're all of us foolish enough to like to retain some illusions of superiority, even if it's only in the matter of height. What was your impression of these people?'

'Of the girl, nothing. The men, I thought, were tough guys and even one day – when we were alone together, Edward – I ventured to tell Tengrala that I didn't think he was altogether wise in his choice of companions. He just said "they are of use to me", and the subject was never mentioned again. I didn't speak to him of the fair girl, of course.'

'What do you think of that, Mr Adams?'

'I think my client should have told me that a key to his apartment was in someone else's possession. As to the rest . . . I don't know what to make of it, Mr Maitland.'

'Talk to him again, Mr Adams. Perhaps now you know so much, he will be more open with you.'

'He has told you – ?' Antony was silent. 'Yes, I see he has been more open with you than he was with me,' said Edward Adams slowly. 'Well, well, I will take your advice.'

'I told him quite frankly that his lawyer was more deserving of his confidence than I could ever be,' said Antony. 'And I think perhaps I should explain that I am not as convinced as you are of his guilt, I mean to take my inquiries a little further. I should like to think that I have your blessing in this, but I'm afraid my Ambassador's wishes must come first.'

'And very properly. Let me say just this, Mr Maitland, in some way you have made Tengrala trust you, and to my mind he was right to do so. May I ask only that if anything comes to light that would help his defence, in the unhappy event of his going to trial, you will keep me informed.'

'That is my intention. That is why I came to see you first, I shouldn't like you to think that anything underhand was

68

going on so far as you were concerned.'

'You are going to see these people, these friends of Tengrala's?'

'That is my intention, and also perhaps, as you suggested, his father.' He picked up his cup and drained it, and put it down again carefully beside him. 'I have a feeling,' he said, dividing a smile between his host and hostess, 'that this is going to turn out to have been the most pleasant visit in the course of my investigation. I have to thank you both for receiving us so kindly, and not resenting, Mr Adams, what a lesser man might consider interference.'

He came to his feet as he spoke, and both Edward Adams and Roger followed his example. 'There's just one thing,' said the lawyer, for the first time sounding almost tentative. 'If the police hear of your inquiry – ?'

'They can object, of course, I'm sure they will object, but there's nothing they can do about it. Mr Farrell and I have been accorded diplomatic status for the time begin. I understand, too, that His Excellency has referred the matter to your State Department.'

'And all this on behalf of a citizen of one of the Commonwealth countries who has got himself into trouble.' Edward Adams's smile broadened, a thing a moment ago Antony wouldn't have thought possible. 'Well, well, you have your secrets, as in some cases I have mine, and you may be assured I will not urge you to reveal them.'

III

They went back to the hotel to find that Jenny and Meg had already been in and gone out again, leaving a note to say that they were having tea at the Park Plaza. 'We might join them there,' said Roger rather doubtfully, glancing at his watch. But before they could reach any decision, the door of the Farrells' suite burst open and Meg came in, followed at a rather more sober pace by Jenny. 'That pet of a doorman told us you were back,' Meg said. 'Isn't it wonderful that he should remember us out of all the people he sees.'

'People always remember you, Meg,' Roger pointed out to her, which was true enough.

'It's our cute accents,' said Antony seriously. 'I noticed that last time we were here, didn't you, love?'

'I couldn't help it,' said Jenny. 'Have you had tea? They don't make a ceremony of it here, but I expect we could get something from room service. Or is it,' she added, looking rather closely from one of the men to the other, 'too early for a drink?'

'You're quite right, love, a drink is what we need,' said Antony, allowing a certain enthusiasm to invest his tone. 'Not, I dare say, that Meg will think that we deserve one,' he added. 'We aren't much nearer to solving the murder of Peter Ngala.'

'Oh, come now!' Roger sank down into one of the easy chairs as he spoke. 'Meg, will you ring Room Service and order something. If we're going to talk – '

'You're quite right, it had better be here.'

'And as for our not deserving one,' Roger went on, as Meg moved obediently towards the telephone on the desk under the window, 'I think we've done pretty well for one afternoon. At least, Antony has,' he added to Jenny, who had taken another of the chairs. 'If there ever was such a chap for asking questions – '

'You put your oar in once or twice,' Maitland pointed out. 'Did you mind?'

'You know I was grateful. Anyway, Roger, what is this progress we're supposed to have made?'

'We've got the names and addresses of six possible suspects other than Tengrala Nema, one of whom actually had keys to the flat and to the building, and could therefore have taken the spare car keys, not to mention the rifle, at any time.'

'A smashing blonde with somewhat loose morals,' said Antony.

'What on earth do you mean, darling?' demanded Meg, turning from the telephone, her mission accomplished. 'Nobody talks about morals today.'

'It does seem to me that it might be significant,' said Antony meekly, 'that she's living with one man, and carrying on, at the same time, with the youngster whom I have the greatest difficulty in not thinking of as a client.' Meg grimaced. 'Yes, I thought you wouldn't like that,' said Antony teasingly. He knew quite well that she had been brought up in a strict Presbyterian household, and wasn't above reminding her of the fact. 'Anyway, as Roger said, we've got these six names, and we had tea with Tengrala's lawyer and his wife, Hetty and Edward Adams, who live in the same building, and there is no chance of his resenting my meddling, which I must admit is rather a relief.'

'You mean to go on with it then?' said Jenny, putting her finger at once on the point that interested her.

'Yes, love, I'm afraid I must, and this is where Roger isn't altogether in sympathy with me. I'm inclined to believe Tengrala when he says he didn't commit the murder. I don't think Roger is. I'm also inclined to like him, in spite of . . . well, we'll come to that. I don't know whether Roger agrees with me there either.'

'Tell them his story and let them judge,' Roger urged him.

'When the drinks come,' Antony agreed. But the waiter arrived at that moment and he had no further excuse for delay.

'Well, that sounds like fun,' said Meg inappropriately when he had finished. 'I wish I'd met the Adams's. They sound just like the people who should be playing Donald and Gladys Turnstall in *Done in by Daggers*.'

'My dear Meg, he's a lawyer and she's a housewife, and I don't suppose either of them has any acting ability.'

'They'd only have to be themselves, as you described them. Anyway, darling, you're avoiding the point,' said Meg unfairly. 'What do you think – ?'

'If you think you should go ahead, Antony, of course you must,' said Jenny firmly. 'I don't think either Meg or I are in a position to know if you're right or wrong about Tengrala Nema, not having seen him.'

'You would, of course, advise him to do exactly what he intended all along,' said Meg, but she was speaking to Jenny and there was no sharpness in her tone. 'But I agree with you really,' she went on, 'as long as he doesn't try to keep us in the dark.'

'I'll have to talk to the Ambassador first. The position must be put to him squarely before I do anything at all.'

'Will that mean your going to Washington again?'

'No, I don't think so. The telephone will do for what little needs to be said. In fact, if you don't mind, any of you, I'll go up to our room and put the call through now.'

IV

Before he phoned the Embassy Antony spent a little time considering how best to convey Tengrala Nema's confidences to His Excellency in a sufficiently guarded way, going so far as to make some notes to himself, which he then put into his pocket and forgot about. It took a little time to run Sir Huntley to earth but he was found at last and allowed Maitland to have his say without interruption. When he had finished there was dead silence for a moment, so that Antony was beginning to wonder whether after all another trip to Washington would be necessary at this stage, but when the Ambassador spoke it was clear he had had no difficulty in taking in the main parts of the story. 'That's very interesting,' he said then, in a tone that left no doubt that the remark was an understatement. 'Am I to take it you're willing to continue?'

'Certainly, sir, if you wish it.'

'There are reasons,' said His Excellency vaguely. 'We shall have to meet again and I'll explain to you fully then. In the meantime, let me just say that what you've told me makes it all the more important for you to proceed as planned.' His tone sharpened a little. 'Do you understand?'

'No,' said Maitland frankly. 'However, I'll do as you say, of course. It may take a little while though, to see all these people over the holidays. Do you think your old friend is likely to become impatient?'

'That's a chance we have to take. I think myself I can persuade him to hold his hand for a little while at least. Do your best, Antony, that's all I ask.'

'But he's looking for results,' said Maitland ruefully when he rejoined his friends a little later. 'I did my best to convey to him that I wasn't hopeful, but he's obviously relying on my being able to prove who really killed Peter Ngala.'

'You must admit, darling, it's quite in your line.'

'Nothing of the sort. If this were England, if it was a case

73

I was engaged in professionally, that would be different. As it is, why should any of these people even agree to seeing me?'

'Because people love to talk,' said Meg. 'I should have thought you'd learned that by now.'

'Yes, I know, Meg, but ... oh well, who lives may learn. We'll see what we can do tomorrow, Roger, but I decline to interrupt any of these people's Christmas festivities.'

'The question is, Antony,' said Jenny who had been unusually silent, even for her, 'how do you feel about it now that you've seen Tengrala Nema?'

'I think,' said Antony slowly, 'that if this were England and if I were his counsel, I'd accept the brief and do the best I could with it in court, and beyond that leave his affairs strictly alone.'

'Does that mean you think he did it?'

'It means, love, that I don't know. I can't myself see any motive, but with his avowed sympathy for terrorism in what he considers a good cause, who can say what he may have done.'

Jenny seemed satisfied with that answer, but Meg was more insistent. 'This case is different though, isn't it darling?' she asked.

'There's the diplomatic angle involved. I don't think Sir Huntley is one to get the wind up unnecessarily, I'm sure he thinks the situation is potentially dangerous. Even more so now, I gathered, though he could do no more than hint what he meant over the phone.'

'Well, I think it's very noble of you both,' said Meg. 'But hard on Jenny being left alone while I'm busy too.'

'I don't mind,' said Jenny, 'there's lots to see even without going very far from the hotel.' And was immediately overwhelmed with advice from all three of her companions as to

74

where it was safe or not safe to travel alone.

When the pandemonium, which had no appreciable effect on Jenny, had subsided, they all went down to dinner. Conversation then ran on the play and other safe subjects, including that afternoon's visit to the Cloisters, but Antony's mind was obviously elsewhere. 'What were you thinking about?' Jenny asked him later when they were in their own room. 'You liked Tengrala, didn't you? Are you worried about him?'

'Yes, I am. And you're quite right, love, I did like him, though he is potentially dangerous. Who's to say what any of us might do if we'd been brought up in similar circumstances? But what I was thinking about was, who drove the murder car? It looks as if perhaps our first visit tomorrow should be to this Lieutenant Hennessey, to find out some details of the murder.'

'Don't you think he might resent your interference? You said –'

'I'm sure he will, but that oughtn't to be allowed to matter if I can get what I want out of him.'

'No, I see that. But you won't let it spoil Christmas Day, will you, Antony? I've been looking forward so to that,'

'I think I can safely promise you I won't,' Antony told her. 'All these people I want to see will have their own fish to fry that day.'

'Or turkeys to cook, or whatever,' said Jenny. On which lighter note they went to bed.

Monday, 24th December

I

During the night his resolution hardened and he communicated his decision to Roger over breakfast the following morning that they should seek out Lieutenant Hennessey without delay.

'Yes, I think you're right,' said Roger thoughtfully. 'The only thing is that this morning may be the one chance you have of catching Miss Charron alone, and you must admit that she's pretty much a key figure in the case.'

'You mean the man she lives with, Joel Harte, may be at work this morning? I was rather assuming that with Christmas Day coming on a Tuesday – '

'It's worth trying,' said Roger. 'You can hardly ask her about the key to Tengrala's flat with the other man present.'

'No, that's true. We'll try her first then. But after that – '

'We'll beard the lion,' Roger agreed. Meg had left early for her rehearsal with a promise to be back as soon as she could. They left Jenny presently still absorbed in yesterday's Arts and Leisure section of the *New York Times*, in which an interview in depth with Miss Margaret Hamilton was prominently featured.

A visit to the apartment occupied by Margaret Charron and Joel Harte necessitated a journey to Greenwich Village. Both Antony and Roger admitted later to a little surprise when the taxi drew up before an extremely neat house, the woodwork newly painted, the windows shiningly clean. Some of the areas they had driven through hadn't led them to expect so much respectability. 'What are our chances of getting another cab here?' Antony asked the driver as they got out.

The man looked from one to the other of them assessingly for a moment. 'Be glad to wait for you,' he offered.

'That would be helpful.' Maitland closed with the offer immediately. But he added to his friend as they turned away, 'You shouldn't look so prosperous, Roger, he's relying on a big tip.'

'No harm in that,' said Roger cheerfully. 'We're on an expense account, aren't we?'

'I suppose we are,' said Antony, rather startled. The matter had honestly never occurred to him in that light before, nor did he think now that his friend was in the least degree concerned about it. He was examining a double row of bell pushes as he spoke. A house converted into apartments, and each tenant presumably as houseproud as the next. 'Charron and Harte,' he said at last. 'No ambiguity there.'

There was what he took to be a loudspeaker near the double row of bell pushes, but oddly enough it remained silent, only a loud click alerted the more practical Roger that the front door might have been opened for them. He tried it and found that he was right. 'Come along,' he invited.

Inside was a hall with three doors leading off it and a flight of stairs giving access to the higher regions. While they were hesitating a door on the right opened, revealing a blonde young woman who seemed startled to see them. 'Oh!' she

78

exclaimed, 'I thought – '

She broke off there and studied them for a moment. 'What do you want?' she demanded. 'It was you who rang our bell, wasn't it?'

'If you're Miss Charron, it was.'

'I am, but I don't know you.' Her tone indicated that this was a state of affairs with which she was quite content.

'No, of course you don't.' Maitland's voice had taken on a soothing note. 'We're interested – I should stress in a friendly way – in a Mr Tengrala Nema. As I believe he's also a friend of yours, I'm sure you understand our concern.'

'If you're talking about the death of that man Ngala, the police's attitude is absolute nonsense,' she said haughtily. 'But you're not from the police, and I know he chose a black lawyer. Besides, your accent isn't right.'

'I'm sorry about that,' said Antony meekly.

'British, aren't you?'

'We are. My name is Maitland, and this is my colleague Mr Farrell. At the moment we represent the British Embassy, who take a good deal of interest in the possible fate of a former member of the Commonwealth.'

To his relief the answer seemed to satisfy her. 'You'd better come in,' she said grudgingly, and backed away from the door.

'Is Mr Harte at home?' asked Antony, following her. The door led directly into the living room and there was no-one else in sight. Behind him he heard the door close, which he put down to Roger's doing.

'He went shopping. You want to see him as well?'

'Yes, we do, but first, Miss Charron, we'd very much like to have a word with you alone. You'll understand why when I tell you that Mr Nema has to some extent confided in me. Have the police been here?'

'No, why should they?'

'He was obviously not quite so open with them. I'm referring to the keys of his apartment, which he says are in your possession.' He was watching her as he spoke. Indeed she was a very good-looking girl, in her mid-twenties so far as he could judge, well spoken and beautifully dressed.

'Well!' She sat down abruptly. 'I'm surprised at Tengrala,' she said after a moment. 'The fact that I have the keys is nobody's business but his and mine.'

'You'll forgive me, Miss Charron, but if it comes to an arrest it may very well also be his lawyer's business, and so I have advised him.' There seemed no reason to mention that Mr Adams was already acquainted with the fact through Mrs Adams's powers of observation.

'Why?'

'I think you know the reason as well as I do. He tells me they were the only other keys in existence besides his own, and that his own set has never left his possession. The keys to his car were taken, and one of the rifles there ... or perhaps it might be more correct to say "borrowed" since both were returned.'

'That doesn't need explaining. He had access to them, didn't he?'

'A moment ago you were assuring me that the police's attitude was ridiculous. I presume you meant by that, their attitude towards your friend.'

'I said it was ridiculous because they can't arrest him. So why bother?'

'Why can't they arrest him?'

'His father's an ambassador, isn't he?'

'Who has disowned his son. Besides, his lawyer assures me –'

'Well, I told you – or didn't I? – there's nothing I can do

for him. The keys have never been out of my possession either, so it's quite obvious he wasn't telling you the truth.'

'Are you quite sure about that, Miss Charron?'

'Of course I'm sure!'

'May we sit down?'

'I guess so. What else can there be to ask me?' She was at her most abrupt again.

'One or two things,' said Maitland vaguely. 'To begin with, I take it Mr Harte knows nothing of these keys?'

'No, and he mustn't.' She glowered at him and he returned her look with his blandest smile. 'I see,' she said resentfully. 'If I don't answer these questions of yours you'll tell him.'

'I haven't said so, Miss Charron.'

'No, but it's quite obvious what you mean.' Maitland did not reply, and after a moment she went on in a slightly more conciliatory tone, 'As a matter of fact it's none of Joel's business, but on the other hand I'd prefer him not to know.'

'Then we'll hope there'll be no need for him to find out. But first I'd like to clarify the matter a little. Think about it for a moment. Are you quite sure he knows nothing of your visits to Mr Nema?'

'If he did I wouldn't be here.'

'I see.'

'And if he saw the keys accidentally, he'd have no means of identifying them. I haven't got a label on them you know, they're just on my ring with the others.'

'And you're quite sure ... for instance is there anything distinctive about either of them?'

'The key to the apartment has a triangular head, not a round one. But I tell you I've never left my keys about. They're always right at the bottom of my purse ... where I can hardly find them myself,' she added, with the first suspicion of a smile they had seen from her.

'Suppose I was to ask you to swear to that, Miss Charron?'

'It wouldn't do any good, I don't believe in God.'

'When did you see Mr Nema last?'

'I spent the afternoon with him the day before the shooting.'

'How did he seem that day?'

'The same as always. He's a fanatic, Mr Maitland.'

'And since then.'

'It didn't seem wise.'

'To go there alone, you mean? Have you been there in company with others of your friends?'

'Sure. When it was known that the rifles had been found –'

'There were things to discuss, yes, I can see that. How many people besides Mr Nema were in this secret of yours, knew of this plot?'

'Five of us at first, but I told Joel later.'

'Did he approve?'

'He understood the need.'

'And the others?'

'There are three men who are to help in the liberation of Bosegwane.'

'A Frenchman, an Irishman and a German,' said Maitland thoughtfully.

'If you know all about it, why ask me?'

'You mentioned five people as well as yourself, I believe.'

'The other one is Noella. She doesn't count really.'

'Why not?'

'Because she's very feminine.' Her tone poured scorn on the phrase. 'She's in love with Jean – Jean le Bovier – so anything he does must be right.'

'How did you come to be involved with them?'

'Michael looked me up. My work for human rights hasn't

82

gone altogether unnoticed,' she added proudly. 'I think he thought I might be able to act as a – as a sort of recruiting agent, but once I met Tengrala he forbade me absolutely to take anyone besides Joel into my confidence. But for all that, they never excluded me from their conferences, I think I may say my suggestions were well received.'

'I'm sure they were.' There was no mistaking the dryness of Antony's tone, and she challenged him instantly.

'You don't believe in human rights, Mr Maitland?'

'I don't like leading questions,' said Antony, smiling. 'But if you would like to know my exact position in the matter I have to admit that I'm sick to death of the excesses that simple phrase always seems to conjure up.' He left her to think about that for a moment (it was something, after all, to have silenced her) and then asked, 'Have you ever seen anybody at Tengrala Nema's apartment besides these three men and Miss Noella Crashaw?'

'No, I think the six of us are the only people Tengrala knows in New York, except for that fat lawyer and his wife of whom he seems to be rather fond.'

'You say Miss Crashaw is not a convinced terrorist?'

'A war of liberation is a very different thing, Mr Maitland.'

'But the three men . . . are you sure that one of them could not have had the opportunity of extracting the key from your handbag, say, on one of the occasions when you met prior to the murder?'

She paused for a long moment before replying. 'I guess it's possible,' she said at last slowly, 'if one of them had taken the trouble to find out what Tengrala's door keys looked like, and also knew of my association with him.'

'Do you think any of them could have known that?'

'How can I know? Tengrala talked to you.'

83

'That, if I may say so, was rather a different matter. Perhaps you don't quite appreciate the seriousness of his position, Miss Charron.'

'I don't think it's as bad as you make out. They may throw him out of the country, but that won't do him much harm. But why bother with all these questions when the solution is so very simple? The rifles were kept in his apartment, obviously the place where the others live wouldn't be suitable, and the arrangement was made before Joel came in with us. Tengrala had only to take one, and the car, of course, was readily at his disposal.'

'He had also to find a driver.'

'I hadn't thought of that.'

'And as his acquaintance in New York seems to have been restricted, that doesn't give him very much choice, does it?'

'He must have known other people here.'

'As acquaintances only. He says the six of you were the only people who ever visited him, but in fairness I must add, Miss Charron, he was making no accusation when he told me that.'

'He knew the Adamses too.'

'But I don't think they visited him, though he had been to their apartment. In any case,' he smiled suddenly, 'can you imagine Mr Adams ...'

For the first time she returned his smile quite openly. 'No, I can't,' she admitted. And then, 'You look like a sensible man, Mr Maitland, and so does your very silent companion. Wouldn't it be much simpler to accept the obvious?'

'Perhaps I think it's too obvious. Can you give me any suggestion as to what Tengrala Nema's motive could have been for this murder?'

'No, it seems to be a complete contradiction of everything

84

we've discussed. But he may have had reasons none of us knew about.' And as she spoke there was a sound of a key in the lock, the door swung open, and a lanky young man with a bag of groceries stood on the threshold.

'Joel darling,' said Margaret Charron, all trace of her former sulkiness completely lost, 'I've been having such an exciting time. Come and meet two men from the British Embassy.'

Joel Harte had a craggy face that matched his tall bony frame, but his smile seemed quite spontaneous, though it had some surprise in it. 'I can't think what you're doing here or what you could want with Margaret,' he said, 'but whatever it is I hope she was able to help you.'

'It wasn't only Miss Charron we wanted to see,' said Maitland. 'We were hoping you'd get back before too long. My name is Maitland, by the way, and this is my associate, Roger Farrell.'

'Joel Harte,' said the newcomer automatically. 'But I gather you know that already. Do you mind explaining?'

'Of course not. If Miss Charron will forgive us for repeating ourselves. You've heard of the murder of Peter Ngala.'

'Oh that!' Harte responded with a quick frown. 'But Margaret said ... the British Embassy? How can that be your concern?'

'Because the New York police seem to be interested in a man whom I believe is a friend of yours, Tengrala Nema. As a citizen of one of the former Commonwealth countries we have naturally some interest in his welfare.'

Again the rather casual explanation was received without comment. 'And because we're friends of his ... I can understand your interest, but not what we can be supposed to be able to do for you.'

'If you come in, Joel, and put down that bag before it splits

85

and the groceries fall all over the floor,' said Margaret, 'at least these poor men can sit down again and we can all be comfortable.' She watched with an air of indulgence as he followed her directions, and presently all of them were seated. 'They seem to be under the impression that poor Tengrala may not have done the shooting,' she said then. 'At least,' she added with a ravishing smile in Roger's direction, 'Mr Maitland seems to think so. Mr Farrell has been strangely quiet.'

'Of course there must be some explanation,' said Joel. 'You're quite right,' he added, turning to the visitors, 'Tengrala is a friend of ours but he wouldn't be if I thought him capable of an act like that. Cold-blooded murder, in fact.'

'You wouldn't say then that it might be better termed an assassination, and under that title perhaps justified by circumstances?'

'No, I would not.'

'I should tell you, Mr Harte, that Mr Nema has given us an explanation of the rifles in his apartment. He also says that you are one of the people aware of their purpose. That doesn't seem altogether consistent with what you just said.'

'It's perfectly consistent. You say you know what Tengrala intended?'

'To be part of a movement to overthrow the government of his country. Did you know of this?' Maitland asked again.

'Before I answer that I should like some clarification of your own position, Mr Maitland. In what way is your government interesting itself in African affairs?'

'In this case only insofar as it concerns Tengrala Nema's well-being,' said Antony, and wondered as he spoke how far that was true.

'In other words, if you can you'll help him?'

'Precisely.'

'Then perhaps you'll understand my attitude. The situation in Bosegwane has been described to me, and it seems that nothing but good could come from the government being overthrown, even by force. But I think I should point out to you that this plan does not give our friend a motive for killing Peter Ngala.'

'I'm aware of that. You can confirm then that this part of his story, which accounts for the presence of the rifles in his apartment, is true?'

'Yes. Does his lawyer know of this?'

'I believe not, though I have advised Mr Nema to tell him. It isn't the kind of thing that would exactly sound well put forward in court as a defence,' he added smiling.

'I suppose not.' Harte seemed to be relaxed again. 'Is that all you wanted of us?'

'A little more. May I use the word conspiracy without offending you? Miss Charron informs me that besides the two of you four people knew what Mr Nema was about.'

'Yes, that's quite true. I was a latecomer, but for some time now I've sat in at most of their discussions.'

'And nothing was ever said to offend these ideas you have expressed to me?'

Harte frowned for a moment over the question. 'I've been aware, of course, that the three other men concerned are tougher guys than I am. Tougher than Tengrala too, for all that he tried to match them in conversaion. I think that's understandable, they're mercenaries and not ashamed of it, but with no direct stake in the cause for which they would be fighting. As any sane man must, I deplore the necessity for war, though I realise it's sometimes inevitable. I realise too that when it comes things are done not in cold blood but in hot. Perhaps I discounted a little of their talk as boasting, but,

87

no, I can't say that any of it offended me.'

'You say, Mr Harte, that you believe in Mr Nema's innocence. Have you realised what that implies? Somebody entered his apartment and took the keys of his car, and also one of the rifles. What's more, they put both rifle and keys back again later. Can you explain that?'

'I can't. Certainly I've never had the means of entering his building without his knowledge, still less of getting into his apartment, and even more certainly neither has Margaret. But I think you must allow for the possibility that one or more of the three others, who are closer to him in a way than we were, might have been in a position to do the things you say.'

'You're leaving Miss Crashaw out of it.'

'Noella? Yes, of course I am. But were we Tengrala's only friends?'

'According to him, yes. The only ones, at least, to ever visit him. The others who were his friends were the man who is now his lawyer, Edward Adams, and his wife Hetty. I believe Mr Nema has visited them, they live in the same building, but not vice versa.'

'Yes, I've heard him speak of them. He wouldn't encourage visitors, of course, with the rifles there. I can't say I have a very high opinion of my three co-conspirators, Mr Maitland – you see I'm taking up your word – but the same objection applies to them as to Tengrala. What motive could they have for such an act?'

'If Mr Nema is innocent someone had a motive and has tried very hard to frame him, either out of spite or as a mere matter of self-preservation. And may I remind you that not only the person who fired the shot was concerned; somebody drove the car.'

'Yes, of course, that's one of the things I've been wondering

88

about. But I can't help feeling there must be some other explanation.'

'Six people knew the rifles were in the apartment, and also knew Mr Nema's car by sight, I suppose.'

'Yes, but look at it this way. Supposing one of the six – I'd like to exclude myself and Margaret, but I realise that from your point of view that isn't reasonable – supposing one of us talked loosely. The apartment could have been burgled, I believe there are ways of effecting an entry that leave no trace. And the rifle and the car keys could have been put back in the same way after the murder.'

'That's a thought certainly,' said Antony, and did not add that if it were true it would make his task not just a little harder but downright impossible. 'All right, Mr Harte, there's one more question. Have you ever heard anything to suggest to you that one of the three mercenaries you mention might have had access to the apartment, even when Mr Nema wasn't there?'

'No, I've heard nothing to suggest that.'

'Or that any of them wasn't completely in sympathy with Mr Nema's aims?'

'No.'

Antony came to his feet. 'Then we'd better leave you to put away your groceries,' he said. 'I'm grateful to you both for being so helpful. If it should be that we need to see you again, would you be willing?'

'Yes, of course, but what else could you possibly want to ask us?'

'There are other people we are to see. Something may arise from their evidence that you could confirm or deny.'

'Then of course we'll do what we can.' He was already unpacking the bag he had brought in with him, and finding a large jar of instant coffee on top was reminded that no refreshment had been offered to his visitors. 'Margaret dear, don't you think we ought to give these men something to drink?'

'Yes, of course, I should have thought of it before.' But Maitland was now eager to be gone, and Roger willing enough to follow his example. They steadfastly refused all offers of refreshment, and a few moments later were re-entering their faithful cab.

II

The cab driver, by some oversight, actually knew his way to the precinct station out of which Lieutenant Hennessey of the NYPD worked. Antony from his previous visit knew this was the exception for any but the most obvious landmarks, and Roger from the few days he had spent sightseeing was already an old enough hand to realise that they were quite unusually fortunate in this. 'The only thing is,' he said, as the vehicle bumped its way over the innumerable potholes, 'will he be there, and will he see us if he is?'

There was only one answer for that. 'I don't know,' said Maitland. 'We can but try. And I think,' he added with rather less optimism than he had displayed earlier in the day, 'if he does see us it may be an awkward interview.'

In this he was wrong. Lieutenant Hennessey was in, and in spite of the fact that it was nowhere near noon yet seemed to be holding a kind of reception in his office. On their mere request to see him Roger and Antony were immediately added to the party, and it was a full half hour before the rest of the guests departed and they found themselves alone with their quarry.

'Well now, gentlemen,' said Hennessey, 'what would you be after wanting with me?' His accent was pure New York, though even Maitland, with his quick ear for such things, couldn't have identified the district, but they were to find that he was not above affecting an Irish idiom when he chose. He sat back now in the chair behind his desk and regarded them benevolently. There could be no doubt that his mood was mellow, but there was also no doubt that he was very far from having been affected in the slightest degree by what he had drunk.

Antony started the now familiar explanation. 'I realise,' he concluded, 'that this may well seem an unpardonable interference to you. But I hope you will try to understand that Her Majesty's Government feels some anxiety – '

He was interrupted by a ham-like fist raised with the obvious intention of stopping the flow of his apology. 'You wouldn't be thinking now that we might be going to try any of the tricks you read about in books on this young man?' Hennessey was a big man with a round face and a ruddy complexion, and Maitland for one was in no doubt at all that he was of quite formidable intelligence.

'I don't think that at all,' he said and smiled suddenly, 'in the circumstances, in view of his admittedly rather tenuous connection with the Bosegwane Embassy to the United Nations, I don't think you'd dare.'

It was obvious that the chance he had taken had come off. The lieutenant grinned back at him, nodded his head as though in agreement and said reflectively, 'I wonder what it is then that you want?'

'From what little we know it's obvious that you have valid ground for suspicion. However, we're anxious to know the full strength of the case against Mr Nema, and to make sure that he has adequate representation.'

For the moment it seemed that the half truth would be sufficient. 'The full strength of the case against him,' said the detective, still in a pensive mood. 'That's a tall order. As to his representation, I know Edward Adams quite well, he'll not do better.'

'I'm sure you're right. But the thing we're not clear about, Lieutenant, is the exact circumstances of the murder.' Throughout the interview he remembered to adopt the American pronunciation of the detective's title.

'It was extensively reported in all the newspapers.'

'Yes, but I wasn't in the country then.' (Roger had arrived the day after the murder, he knew, but there had been no reason then for him to take any particular notice of what had happened.)

'I thought you said you were attached to the British Embassy.'

'For the time being only.' He smiled again. 'A special duty, as you might call it.'

'Very likely. I'd be interested to know the exact nature of this special duty though.'

'Certainly not to interfere with the course of justice.'

'Then – '

'My – my associate,' said Roger, who'd obviously come to the same conclusion as his friend, that the detective was a man who would react well to truthfulness, 'has some experience in these matters.'

'A private eye?'

'No, no, a lawyer, I think you call it a trial lawyer, Lieutenant. But, as he told you, he has no desire to interfere in any way.'

'Unless of course,' said Hennessey, 'I should regard your

being here at all as interference.' Then he too smiled. 'You don't speak my language as well as your friend, Mr Farrell.'

Roger frowned over that. 'Lootenant,' Antony explained helpfully, hoping as he spoke that that was all that Hennessey meant. He did not add that he had a natural gift for mimicry which led him quite innocently into difficult corners sometimes. 'I think what's troubling you,' he added to the detective, 'is what we intend to do with any information you may give us.'

'You're right there.'

'And the answer is, at this stage I can't tell you. Not because I won't, but because quite literally I can't. Let me counter with a question of my own, Lieutenant. Supposing you were given proof of Tengrala Nema's innocence, how would you feel about that?'

'Have you some reason for thinking him innocent?'

'My answer to that must be that at present I have only his word for the fact. My own feelings about it ... but they're beside the point.'

'You've seen Tengrala Nema then?'

'We both have.'

'Did he complain of ill treatment?'

'Not a word. Let me remind you that the idea of such a complaint was yours, not ours.'

'You do intend to undertake some sort of investigation?'

'So far as it is in our power. We haven't the police's facilities even if we were in England, and here, of course, we depend solely on your goodwill.'

'Hm.' Hennessey considered again and then smiled at them impartially. 'Very neat,' he commented. 'I'm to tell you what I know, and if you discover anything ...'

'I might not consider myself free to disclose what I have

93

found out to you.'

'Unless they were facts favourable to your . . . shall we say to your protégé?'

'Precisely.' (Roger glanced at his friend, thinking that if Meg had been present she would have protested, 'Darling you're getting exactly like Uncle Nick!' But Antony was far too absorbed at the moment to have room in his mind for anything beyond what he obviously considered the examination of a witness who needed particularly careful handling.)

'That's honest, at any rate.' Hennessey ruminated again. 'I've not decided, mind you, but tell me what you want to know and we'll see.'

'Only what happened outside the United Nation's building a week ago last Friday. The fourteenth of December, wasn't it?'

'Murder, assassination . . . whatever you like to call it. And when you say outside . . . we'll come to that in a minute. That is, if you're as persistent as I think you're going to be,' he added, rather ruefully.

'About the murder we know.' Maitland's tone had taken on a little dryness. 'We know too that the victim was one Peter Ngala who headed the United Nation's delegation from Timkounou. But there must have been witnesses. The question is, what did they say?'

'According to what Mr Farrell told me your profession will have given you some knowledge of police work, Mr Maitland.'

'Indirectly, yes.'

'Then you won't be surprised if I tell you that no two statements tallied completely with one another.'

'I'm not surprised at all. As you can imagine, Lieutenant Hennessey, when I'm in court I can sometimes turn that fact

94

to my advantage. But I do appreciate that it can be very annoying from your point of view.'

Hennessey's answering smile was a little absent this time. 'I needn't trouble you with the various descriptions of the car, since we were pretty sure by the time all the statements were taken we had the right license plate. Oddly enough, though only one man was sure of the entire number, others had noticed how it began, others how it had ended. It seemed fairly certain that the full number we had been given was correct. At that point, of course, Mr Nema's statement that the car was missing was sufficient explanation. We wondered a little that he hadn't reported the matter, but foreigners, as you know, are sometimes a little nervous in their dealings with the police.'

'And yet you went ahead with a search of his flat . . . apartment, I should say.'

'That was after the car was found and an examination of it seemed to confirm that it was indeed the one used in the murder. I gather you know what our search disclosed. But you were asking me about the events on the afternoon of the fourteenth.'

'Yes that's what interests me most at the moment.'

'Are you familiar with the United Nations building, Mr Maitland?'

'I've never been inside. When I was here a few years ago I was driven past it, that's all. Perhaps, Roger, it was one of the sights you took in before we arrived?'

'Yes, but like you we didn't venture inside. I understand however, Lieutenant, that what was done took place on First Avenue.'

'You're quite right, the exact layout of the building is completely unimportant. What does matter is that Mr Ngala

95

always walked back to the Timkounou Embassy, coming out of the main entrance and turning south along the sidewalk. As there was no meeting that day we can only assume he had been working in his office, as was also his habit, and perhaps that he had been followed by someone with enough patience to await their opportunity.

'That seems likely. What time did he arrive?'

'At two thirty-eight precisely. And to anticipate your next question, he passed through the main gate at precisely three minutes after four.'

'And then?'

'We are back to assumption again, but this time on a little surer ground. There is one place the car could have been parked, outside the ConEd building – '

'Consolidated Edison,' put in Maitland helpfully to Roger.

' – where some roadwork is going on, so that it wouldn't be in anyone's way. It would also look as if it belonged to someone connected with the operation. Several people think they saw a car there but they didn't notice it particularly, why should they? You may have remarked, Mr Farrell, if you've been here for a few days, that the traffic at this time of the year is very heavy; in fact, I sometimes think it's one long traffic jam from Thanksgiving to Christmas. But however it may have been at the precise moment when Mr Ngala came out, the driver of the car would obviously have been able to see him when he neared the corner, which would give him plenty of time to get out of his parking place and allow his passenger to pick off his mark as Mr Ngala was waiting to cross the road.'

'Risky,' Antony commented.

'Not so risky as you think. There is a bus lane: an ideal escape route.'

'So it would seem. To go back a little, Lieutenant, it's quite certain there were two men in the car?'

'Quite certain. There were various estimates of the speed at which it was travelling after the shooting, which is when the passers-by began to take notice, but that's only what I would have expected. However, everyone agrees that it went on without pause, and the only explanation is that there was a passenger who fired at Mr Ngala.'

'Two people,' said Maitland thoughtfully. 'And one of them a damned good shot. Do you have any idea who the second one might have been?'

Hennessey smiled. 'If the answer to that were yes, Mr Maitland, I'm afraid I couldn't answer it. However, in the absence of Mr Nema's co-operation I haven't been able to get any line at all on his associates in New York.'

'I see. No descriptions from the passers-by?'

'It all happened too quickly. Nobody started taking notice until the shots had been fired, why should they?' he asked again.

'Why indeed?' replied Antony. He got to his feet as he spoke and Roger was quick to follow his example. 'There are certain other questions I should like to ask you, Lieutenant Hennessey,' Maitland said, 'but I'm quite sure you wouldn't feel it was proper to answer them. I hope you realise we're grateful for your courtesy in bearing with us for so long.'

Hennessey lumbered to his feet. 'And you're going on from here to pursue your enquiries?' he asked.

'We'll try not to get in your way,' said Antony, at the same time making a mental note to keep a wary eye out for any of the Lieutenant's men who might have been told to follow them.

'That wasn't exactly what I had in mind. The enquiries

I've made all tend in one direction, and I think you know what that is.'

'Besides circumstantial evidence, which may, as you know, be misleading, there is also the question of motive. Have you been as successful there?'

'In trying a case in England, is it essential for motive to be proved?' asked Hennessey curiously.

'Legally, no. But the jurors are laymen, not lawyers.'

'That's true. It is also true that the two African countries, Bosegwane and Timkounou are not always on the best of terms.' He paused hopefully, but Antony was silent. 'You must have some reason for thinking these enquiries of yours may be successful,' the detective went on.

'That's putting it too strongly. Though I would ask you to reflect on the fact that it's unlikely that Tengrala Nema has had the opportunity of becoming a crack shot.' He began to move towards the door but turned to smile again at Hennessey. 'You remind me, Lieutenant, of a certain Detective Chief Inspector Sykes of Scotland Yard who can never be convinced that I don't know more than I'm telling him.'

'In this case,' said Hennessey bluntly, 'I think you do.'

'Perhaps. But let me remind you that I told you at the beginning of this conversation there were things I wasn't willing to be open with you about. But I *am* grateful, and if we're lucky . . . we shall look forward to meeting you again.'

III

They got back to the hotel and found Jenny just on the point of going to lunch. 'Meg thought she might be back,' she told them, 'but it doesn't look now as if she will be until a bit later on. Anyway, if we go down she'll know where we are.'

Meg and Roger being by this time something in the nature of the oldest inhabitants, a corner table had been kept for them by the window. 'Did you manage to see any of Tengrala's friends?' asked Jenny, when the waiter had taken their order for sherry, not on the rocks, and gone away to stand over the barman while he executed it.

'Two of them,' Antony told her. That day there were few people in the dining-room and they were well isolated from any possibility of being overheard.

'Only two?'

'Yes, but I think we were lucky. Chance gave us sufficient time with Miss Charron alone before Mr Harte came in, so we were able to ask her about the keys, and then he came back and we talked to them both together about less dangerous subjects. A nice chap as a matter of fact, I liked him.'

'What about her?'

'A very beautiful woman, very modern. The sort of person, love – you may find this difficult to understand – who has to have some cause or other to devote herself to.'

Jenny had a smile for that. 'You think I find that difficult to understand. When you go from one – what's Geoffrey's phrase? – one damned crusade to another?' (And when you, thought Roger, who had a particularly soft spot for both of them, have found your cause in devoting yourself to him.)

'That's altogether different.' Maitland was for the moment a little taken aback, as a man might be if a pet lamb turned and bit him. 'What I do for a client is one thing, but at least I don't go around talking about human rights.'

'You wouldn't say trying to help Tengrala Nema had become something of a crusade, I suppose?'

'I took it on to oblige Sir Huntley, who succeeded in making the whole thing sound frightfully important. When

99

I reported what Tengrala had told me he seemed to think it more important than ever. I don't understand that I'm afraid.'

'I think I do,' said Roger, but Jenny didn't give him time to elaborate on that remark.

'But would you be going on with it just for that reason?' she insisted. 'Isn't it because you like him and think he's innocent?'

'I like him and think he *may* be innocent,' Antony corrected her. 'And perhaps you're right, love, but I don't think my motives matter.' He paused a moment while the drinks arrived, satisfactorily free from ice, and then turned his attention to Roger. 'What's all this about understanding what Sir Huntley meant?' he demanded.

'It isn't considered desirable for Timkounou to invade Bosegwane, but I gather from what you've said that nobody approves of the present government of King Mbongo.'

'No, but there's the possibility of Russian intervention. I explained that to you.'

'You've explained it,' Roger agreed, 'and I dare say you were a good deal clearer about it than H.E. was when he told you. All the same, correct me if I'm wrong, I also gathered that there'd be no intervention without a good excuse.'

'I think that was implied.'

'Is the present government of King Mbongo pro-communist? What names these people have,' he added irrelevantly.

'Not that I ever heard. He's just a petty tyrant who doesn't seem to care that his people are starving.'

'So if his government was overthrown?'

'I see what you mean. A revolution from within might not provide our friends with the excuse they want, but it might provide Bosegwane with a much more enlightened government.'

'Which would not displease Westminster, or Washington for that matter.'

'No, I think you're right. All the same, Roger, you must see it complicates matters.'

'I don't see why. The internal affairs of Bosegwane are nothing to do with you.'

'I suppose not.' Maitland spoke slowly, thinking it out. 'But I've never had a client before – and I can't help thinking of Tengrala in that light though I know he isn't – who would celebrate being got off the hook by going out and starting a revolution.'

'Nothing to do with you,' said Roger again.

'No. I suppose I must take Sir Huntley's word for it, that finding who murdered Peter Ngala, provided it isn't the chief suspect, would be for the greater good.'

'I don't think I like politics,' said Jenny reflectively.

'Do you want me to throw in my hand, love?'

'No.' She sounded doubtful, but then she seemed to make up her mind. 'You liked Tengrala,' she said, 'and if he's innocent it must be dreadful for him to be suspected. Besides this King Mbongo doesn't sound to me at all a nice person.'

Antony and Roger exchanged a grin at that, for it was rare indeed for so uncharitable a remark to be heard from Jenny. 'As long as we have your blessing, love,' said Antony mildly, 'I'll tell you – shall I? – just what we've been doing this morning.'

'Yes, do that,' said Jenny putting down her empty glass and preparing to listen.

'It's not all that interesting,' Antony warned her, 'though we had a talk with a lieutenant of the New York Police

Department which was not unilluminating.'

Jenny's eyes widened as he spoke. 'I should have thought he'd have hated you for interfering,' she said.

'Nothing of the sort, though you have to remember, love, it wouldn't have mattered really if he had. No, on the contrary, he was full of the Christmas spirit or something and received us most graciously. As for the rest,' – he was speaking more slowly now – 'there was just one point.' The sentence trailed into silence there, and when he went on it was much more briskly with a factual account of their morning's activities.

IV

Meg came in just as they were finishing their meal. 'I'm absolutely famished, darlings, but I really do think things are getting into shape at last.'

'Are you two going out again?' asked Jenny. 'I'll stay and watch you eat, Meg, and then there's a French film in that little cinema across the road which would keep us occupied for a little while if you like.'

'The park's across the road,' Meg objected.

'I mean, round the corner, the other way. Not very far to walk, and when we come out it will be dark and we can look at the lights along Fifth Avenue.'

'That sounds fine. The question is, what has been going on this morning?'

'Jenny will tell you,' Roger said, a promise Jenny's husband would hesitate to have made, as she wasn't known for lucid exposition. 'My question is, when is this slavedriver of yours going to want you again?'

'On Boxing Day, darling, only they don't call it that here. I really think he might have gone on till midnight tonight only everybody was having a party as soon as they got off the stage, so it turned out not to be much good.'

'I thought you said things were getting nicely into shape.'

'So they are. If Jenny's to tell me about your adventures, I suppose that means you're going out again.'

Roger glanced at Antony who said, 'I'm afraid so,' apologetically. And then, 'I've been thinking though, Roger, shouldn't we try to see Tengrala's father?'

'If you're proposing to warn him you won't be popular with H.E.'

'I thought we decided it was none of our business.'

'That's exactly what I meant.'

'No, I'm curious I suppose. And if he's been keeping a sort of an eye on his son's doings he may be able to tell us something about these friends of his.'

'That's not very likely. Tengrala seemed to imply that there'd been no communication between them at all.'

'Yes, I know. All the same – '

'All the same, you want to do it your way,' said Roger resignedly. 'How do we set about getting an appointment with an ambassador at short notice anyway?'

'A little very tactful telephoning. I'm assuming from their names – I should have asked Tengrala about this – that they won't be celebrating Christmas, so this may not be more than another working day for them. And there's this to be said for it,' he added persuasively, when Roger still looked unconvinced. 'If Hennessey *is* having us followed it won't tell him a thing.'

'Is he likely to do that?'

'I would if I were he.'

'But his men don't know us by sight.'

'He could have had the whole thing arranged by the time

we left the building.'

As regards the celebration of Christmas, events proved Antony right. For whatever reason, Mr Louga Nema agreed to see them provided they would present themselves at the apartment which was now the Bosegwane Embassy within half an hour. This was not too difficult, as unlike his opposite number from Timkounou he had not chosen the vicinity of the United Nations building for his residence, and the walk wasn't much further than the one Jenny proposed to the cinema, though in the opposite direction.

Afterwards Antony and Roger agreed that a tableau had been arranged for their edification, of a hardworking diplomat at work at his desk with a mound of papers waiting for his attention. Louga Nema did not look up immediately when they were announced, and when he did, though his words of welcome were courteous no smile lightened his gravity. 'I am Louga Nema,' he said, and consulted a card in front of him before he went on. 'Mr Maitland, Mr Farrell, representatives of Her Majesty's Government, I bid you welcome. Pray sit down, gentlemen.'

His command of the language was as good as his son's, though slightly more formal. The two visitors seated themselves. 'We're interrupting your work, sir, but we promise we won't keep you long,' Antony assured him. 'It's just that we felt it proper to advise you that as a member of the Commonwealth family of nations everything possible will be done to assure justice for your son.'

'I have sons,' Mr Nema acknowledged, 'in my own counry. They are not, so far as I know, in any difficulty.'

'Tengrala – '

'Is no son of mine. As soon as he came here without my permission.'

'Had you any reason for withholding that permission, sir?'

'I do not like his ideas.' Suddenly he became confidential. 'America is a great country, and her goodwill is important to us. If Tengrala talks freely of his ideas, which are frankly seditious, it could do no good at all.'

'But the murder of Peter Ngala – '

'Has he been accused of that?' asked Mr Nema quickly.

'No, sir, but I think you are aware of the circumstances.'

'Certainly I am. There have been people here, representatives of the United States Government. I think, frankly, that they would have been relieved if I had put forward a plea for diplomatic status for him.'

'If you'll forgive the question, why did you not do so?'

Louga Nema thought for a moment. 'It would have been a lie,' he said, 'and lies as you know are very often necessary in diplomatic matters. But to get him out of the country on such an excuse would have been to admit his guilt.'

'Which you don't accept?'

'As to that, I am afraid the evidence is against him,' said Nema casually. 'Besides, I cannot regret the death of Peter Ngala, the people of Timkounou are enemies . . . our hereditary enemies I believe you'd say. But their president, Joseph Ngala, would be glad enough of an excuse to invade our territory. Tengrala should have thought of that before he acted.'

This repetition of what Sir Huntley had said to him took Antony aback a little. Mr Nema's intelligence service, or perhaps his own native intelligence, would seem to be in excellent working order. 'If you believe in your son's guilt,' he said flatly, 'you must also, I think, have some idea of what could have prompted him to such an act.'

'I have told you I have no son in this country.'

'Very well then, do you know of any connection between Peter Ngala and Tengrala?'

'I would not think it surprising for him to become friendly with an enemy of our people.'

'If that were the case, why should he then resort to murder?'

'Friends fall out.'

'But do you know positively of any such connection?'

'I do not. I do not trust the Ngalas. But this I will tell you, Tengrala was getting money from somewhere, not from me.'

'And you know nothing of his doings during the time he's been here? Or of his companions?'

'Nothing at all. I tell you he is no longer my son and I have no interest in his affairs. But something else I will tell you, it is unlikely if there is no woman in his life.'

'Have you seen him since he arrived in New York?'

'I sent for him when first I heard he was here, but he did not come.'

'I see.'

'He was afraid of my questions, I have no doubt, for whatever he is doing here no good could come from it. I'm sorry, gentlemen.' He rose to his feet as he spoke, 'I am unable to help you, and as you see,' – he waved a hand at the papers on his desk, – 'I'm much occupied.'

'Then we must be all the more grateful that you've given us so much of your time,' said Antony, rising in his turn. 'Particularly as the subject of our discourse must have been distasteful to you.'

'You misunderstand, Mr Maitland. I have received you as a courtesy due from the representative of one Commonwealth country to those of another. The matter of which we have spoken is of no more concern to me than it would be if I read in the newspaper of the affairs of a stranger.'

'But I don't think that was true,' said Roger as they walked back to the hotel. 'I don't know if you agree with me, Antony, but I think he was worried sick about that son of his but too proud to say so.'

'Oh, I agree with you. I wonder, you know, if that chap we just left is really as devoted to the affairs of his king as his son thinks he is.'

'I don't see how we can know that.' Roger smiled. 'You might have tried him with one of your direct questions, but if what you suspect is true you certainly wouldn't have got a direct answer.'

'No, I don't suppose so. I wonder though – '

'What now?'

'I wonder whether there might not be some way of getting father and son together again.'

'Not unless you can persuade Louga to join Tengrala's rebellion,' said Roger. 'And quite honestly. Antony, I don't see how you'd set about that, even if you thought it was the right thing to do.'

'That wasn't quite what was in my mind,' said Maitland thoughtfully. 'Shall we get a cab, Roger, and go down to the Village again, but by a circuitous route this time? Jenny and Meg won't be expecting us just yet.'

'That's all right by me,' said Roger, 'but I didn't think –'

'Don't turn round. Hennessey did put a man on to shadow us, I didn't think he'd miss so obvious an opportunity.'

'Well, as you said, our visit to Louga Nema wouldn't tell him much. But now – '

'Quite simple.' Antony's tone was airy. 'We go into the hotel, take the lift as if we were going up to our rooms, get off

107

half way and come down the emergency stairs.'

'But this isn't one of those hotels with multiple exits,' Roger objected.

'All the better. As long as our escort has the front door under observation he'll be quite happy. I admit it isn't a trick we can try twice.'

'What trick?' demanded Roger, exasperated.

'Going out through the kitchens. The denizens of the nether regions may be surprised, but they won't try to stop us. All right?'

'It's your party,' said Roger helplessly.

The plan went smoothly, but this time their luck was out. After a tedious journey through heavy traffic in a cab whose shock absorbers had obviously given up the struggle long since they found the address they had been given, an apartment in a ramshackle building not far from the more elegant one in which Joel Harte and Margaret Charron lived. There were no bells in evidence but the front door was open and there was nothing to stop them from going upstairs until they found a door on the top floor with the name Crashaw beside it. But despite repeated hammering there was no reply. The only bit of luck about the whole undertaking was that they had asked the taxi to wait.

That night they went to the opera, the Metropolitan Opera House being one of the few places of entertainment that does not choose Monday night for its closing. They dined later at a place nearby, not particularly elegant but with a fantastically long menu, and got back to the hotel sleepy and relaxed. 'And no rehearsals tomorrow,' said Meg. 'It will be a wonderful day, Roger darling.' Which pleased her husband so much that he forbore to retort that her continued preoccupation with the theatre was no-one's decision but her own.

Tuesday, 25th December

I

The first inkling they had that the day was not to go entirely to specification was when they came back from breakfast, which they all took together in the dining-room, predictably late. It was a brisk morning, just the day for a quick walk in the park, and Roger and Meg had gone to their own suite to wrap up warmly. When Antony and Jenny got to their floor and started towards their own room at the end of the corridor they found the trolley with the chambermaid's familiar paraphernalia three doors away, and the girl herself popped out when she heard them and said with an air of congratulation, as though on Christmas Day it was a thing that couldn't be expected, 'The man came to fix your toilet, madam. He says there's nothing wrong with it now.'

'But – ' started Jenny, and broke off, glancing enquiringly at Antony.

'He said your husband had phoned the office to report it out of order,' the girl assured her.

'There must be some mistake.'

'I'm not so sure about that, love,' said Antony quickly. 'Did you know the man?' he asked the chambermaid. 'Is he one of the regular service staff?'

'I'd never seen him before, but that's not surprising. I just thought he was unlucky like me, drawing duty today.'

'Yes, that seems the most likely thing. Is there anything to take you back into our room?' Maitland asked.

'The towels – ' she began.

'Never mind about the towels until later on. I shall be doing some very confidential work and I don't want to be disturbed,' he improvised quickly. 'Jenny love, I don't want even you around. Will you go down to Roger and Meg and stay with them until I come?'

'Antony – '

'Not now, Jenny, I'll explain when I come.'

'Is there something wrong, sir?' asked the chambermaid, not unreasonably.

'Not a thing in the world. Just do as I say, there's a good girl. Please love,' he added seeing a rather mulish expression descending on his wife's usually serene face.

Jenny looked at him for a long moment and then turned on her heel. 'And tell Roger and Meg not to go near their bathroom,' he called after her.

When he disappeared into their own room the maid was still standing staring after him. He thought ruefully that he had not done much to reassure her, but time was of the essence and he didn't know what else he could have said. He made straight for the bathroom, shiningly clean after the chambermaid's ministrations but still towel-less as she had said, and very gently lifted the lid from the tank behind the lavatory. Having seen all he needed he didn't replace it, but leaned it against the side of the bath. A moment later he was dialling the hotel operator to ask to be put through to the police at the nearest precinct.

The request seemed to fluster her. 'Sir, if there's been a robbery – ' she began.

'Nothing like that.'

' – I ought to tell the manager first,' she concluded, not seeming to take in what he was saying.

'It's rather too urgent for that, and nothing for which the hotel can be blamed,' he assured her. 'Put me right through, then you can tell the manager if you like. I'm sure he'll agree that you did the right thing.'

'Very well, sir.' She still sounded doubtful, and he was quite sure she would accept his suggestion at the earliest moment, but an instant later he had forgotten all about that on finding himself connected to a gruff masculine voice announcing itself as Sergeant Duffy.

'My name's Maitland. My wife and I are staying in room 1104 at the Hotel Majestic. This isn't a hoax call and if you're in any doubt about my bona fides the British Ambassador in Washington will vouch for me. I've just discovered a bomb in my lavatory tank ... in my toilet,' he corrected himself. 'It's wired to go off when the system is flushed. There's a possibility the same thing may have been done in a friend's suite at the same hotel, but I've sent my wife to warn him not to go near the bathroom. Can you tell me what my next move should be?'

Perhaps there was something in his manner that the man at the other end of the line found reassuring, perhaps it was his mention of His Excellency. In any case, Sergeant Duffy answered promptly, 'Is there any immediate danger?'

'Not unless the lavatories are flushed, and I assure you I don't intend to allow that to happen. But I'm not competent to dismantle the thing.'

'Leave it to me then, sir. Room 1104, you said?'

'Yes, and my friend's name is Farrell and his suite is easy to remember, 4011. Is there anything you want me to do?'

'Not a thing, sir, except that I should like you to be around when we arrive. There will be a few questions.'

'I'll be here.'

Again Sergeant Duffy seemed to find his tone convincing. 'The place will have to be cleared while the bomb squad are working,' he said, 'but you'd better leave that to us.' And rang off without further delay.

To Antony's relief, though the trolley was still in the corridor the chambermaid had disappeared when he went out of his room, locking the door carefully behind him. However, before he reached the elevator a resplendent personage emerged, whom he took, rightly as it turned out, to be the hotel manager. 'If you're looking for the occupant of Room 1104,' said Antony, 'here I am. I'd advise you not to go any nearer.'

'If you have some complaint, Mr Maitland – '

'No complaint at all, as long as you don't hold me up now. Come with me if you like, I'm going to my friends' suite on the fourth floor. I don't know if you've met Mr and Mrs Farrell.'

'Indeed I have, and I'm very honoured that Miss Hamilton should be staying with us.' There was a visible thawing at the mention of Meg's name. 'But I don't understand – '

'You don't need to just yet,' said Antony, who all this while had been holding the elevator door open. 'Get in, there's a good chap, I'll explain when we get to their room.'

After that things moved quickly. Antony, who had no experience of the New York Police Department, could not but admire the smoothness with which they dealt with the situation. It is true that they verified his statement before setting the wheels in motion, but he had expected that and

112

considered it in the circumstances more than reasonable. They found, of course, that everything was as he had told them, and that for good measure Roger and Meg's bathroom had been similarly booby-trapped.

Of the four of them it was Roger who was at first the most visibly shaken. 'It might have been Meg,' he kept saying, and seemed to find no comfort in Antony's assurance that it probably wouldn't have mattered which of the two of them had triggered the mechanism. But that was later, after the police had ordered the building cleared, and the manager – obviously a resourceful man – had conjured up from somewhere a fleet of luxury buses in which he invited his patrons to take a tour of the town. Jenny and Meg unwillingly went with them, but Antony and Roger, aware that they might be needed, shivered outside with the staff until the all-clear was given and they were at liberty to enter the warm lobby again.

The manager was awaiting them, not quite so deferential as before. 'In my office, gentlemen,' he invited. 'The police – ' and broke off as though the word were an imprecation too foul to be uttered.

The police, however, in the persons of a lieutenant and a sergeant with long unpronounceable names, were courtesy itself. Introductions took place. 'Well, Mr Maitland,' said the senior of the two, 'Sergeant Duffy phoned the British Embassy as you suggested, and it seems the two of you have diplomatic status for the time being. We wouldn't want to go into any matters that might embarrass you, but you must realise that this has left us rather at a loss. It isn't usual for visitors to this country to be subjected to attacks of this kind – '

'Unless they are themselves in some way connected with

113

organised crime,' Maitland finished for him, smiling.

'Something like that was in my mind,' the Lieutenant admitted.

'And very naturally so. Unfortunately I can give you no explanation, though I think you have a right to be told how we've been occupying ourselves for the last few days.' He went on to give the expurgated version of their activities that he had already supplied to Lieutenant Hennessey the day before.

'So Hennessey knows all about this,' the Lieutenant remarked when he had finished.

'He does, but I'd be the first to admit that it's no explanation of what's just happened.'

'No, that's a mystery. Who knows you're in this country, Mr Maitland?'

It was Roger who answered. 'The entire cast of the play my wife's appearing in, I should think,' he said. 'But they could have no reason – '

'No, I agree. Where politics are concerned I don't think one has to look any further. About this mission of yours ... Tengrala Nema – '

'The difficulty is that no-one could have known where we were staying.'

'You're forgetting, Antony,' Roger put in. 'There was some publicity about our arrival, and about yours too.'

'I remember,' said the Lieutenant. 'So you're that Maitland,' he added looking at Antony curiously. 'A lawyer.'

'I'm afraid so.' There was no need to sound apologetic, but for some reason the words came out that way.

'And you don't think you brought the trouble with you?'

'No, I don't.'

'But anyone who was interested could have found out quite

easily where you were staying?'

'If he'd kept his old newspapers.'

'People don't usually throw them out immediately. Anyway, as I say, it's a possibility. So we come to the question of who knew you were interesting yourself in this young man's affairs.'

'Sir Huntley, of course. Somebody whose name I don't know at the State Department. Lieutenant Hennessey. Tengrala Nema and his father, and his lawyer, a Mr Adams. And two friends of his.'

'I don't think you need go any further. It's unlikely that either the Ambassador to the United Nations or young Nema's lawyer have anything to do with it. But are you quite sure he appreciated your intervention?'

'If he resented me he gave no sign of it.'

'Still you'll find that's the answer. I won't bother you gentlemen any more for the moment but I think this is a matter on which I should co-operate with Lieutenant Hennessey, and he may wish to see you himself.'

'Wait a bit! Even if we admit Tengrala's guilt, for the purpose of argument only, having committed one crime doesn't necessarily mean that he was responsible for the attempt on our lives.'

'And on those of Meg and Jenny,' Roger reminded him.

'I h-haven't f-forgotten.' To Roger the quick, angry stammer was as eloquent as a thousand words would have been. 'Did the bomb disposal men tell you, Lieutenant, how much explosive was involved?'

'Enough to ensure that nobody in your room would have been left alive,' said the Lieutenant in a matter-of-fact way. 'Or in yours either, Mr Farrell,' he said.

'I thought so. And how do you think Tengrala could have

got hold of it, Lieutenant?'

'How did he get hold of the rifles in his apartment?'

'Yes, I suppose it's natural that you should think that way. All right, talk to Hennessey. Meanwhile, Roger, I think we'd better see the manager about changing our rooms if that's possible, and giving instructions to the switchboard that no information as to the new numbers is to be given out.'

'It would be nice to get that settled before the girls come back,' said Roger, 'but I don't somehow think he's loving us very much.'

That was undoubtedly true. All the same, with the police gone and the hotel made safe for his returning guests, not to mention the renewed activity in the kitchens, the manager was inclined to be gracious. 'I'm afraid we can't give you another suite, Mr Farrell,' he said, 'but there are two adjoining double rooms on the tenth floor, if those would suit you and your friends.'

'They'll be ideal. And, of course, we'll pay you the same rates as long as we're here,' Roger promised, which did a good deal to improve the atmosphere still further. 'How long will those buses of yours be?' he added.

'Another half hour. If you gentlemen want to make the move before your wives return I'll send two chambermaids to help you. The new numbers are 1001 and 1002. I'm sure you'll find them in every way satisfactory.'

'I'm sure we shall,' Roger assured him. 'But don't forget to impress upon the switchboard – '

'I'll attend to it immediately.' But first he escorted them to the elevator himself and watched them start for their respective rooms.

Twenty minutes later the move was accomplished, with the Farrells in the corner room and the Maitlands next door.

Roger was tapping on the door before Antony had satisfied himself that everything would be to Jenny's liking. 'I thought at first you were taking all this rather calmly,' he said as his friend let him in.

'I'm p-perfectly c-calm,' said Antony, stuttering badly now. More than with anyone else of his acquaintance he would let himself go in front of Roger, and now there was no further need for pretence, no officials to impress with an air of calm trustworthiness. 'I'm perfectly c-calm,' he repeated, 'and I mean to s-see the joker who d-did this in h-hell before I'm through.'

'Yes, I thought you would say that, and I needn't tell you I'm with you all the way,' said Roger imperturbably. 'But what is Jenny going to say?'

'You know Jenny. She won't say anything at all, and I shall feel a h-heel because I'm hurting her. But whoever did this isn't going to get away with it, Roger. To be so completely c-callous as not to care whether Jenny or Meg were killed too ... I think you'd better keep out of it though.'

'Not on your life. I've just as much cause to be angry as you have.'

'But Meg – '

'Do you think she'd want me to sit by while you try to see this thing through on your own?'

'No, I suppose not. All the same – '

'She'd lose all respect for me,' said Roger, 'and I'm not having that.' And as it happened when Meg and Jenny returned and were introduced to their new quarters there was no argument from either of them.

Jenny, as was customary with her, took what had happened quietly, and it was quite clear that the idea of her husband giving up the task he had undertaken never entered her head. Meg was much more vocal about the whole affair, but she too seemed to take her husband's continued participation for granted. 'But do you think it could have been Tengrala?' she demanded, when Roger had sent for drinks from room service.

'If I knew who it was I wouldn't be sitting here,' Antony pointed out. He had himself in command now, so far as outward appearances were concerned. 'But no, I don't think it was Tengrala.'

'His father then? He may have resented what you were trying to do because he's disowned his son.'

'In a way it is a better suggestion, but – '

'If you're going to tell me that ambassadors to the United Nations don't do things like that,' said Meg, 'you're wasting your breath. He must have any one of a dozen minions who would have done it for him.'

'Yes, but I think for all his talk he's really concerned about Tengrala.'

'You're working on the assumption,' said Roger, 'that Tengrala is innocent and that one of his friends tried to frame him.'

'Doesn't that seem obvious?'

'*If* he's innocent that's what must have happened. But the trouble is, Antony, we've only seen two of them.'

'Yes, and that's why my thoughts are running rather strongly at the moment in the direction of Mr Joel Harte.'

'It would explain something else too,' said Roger. 'Margaret Charron is his girl-friend – '

'Really, darling, that's a very common way of putting it,' said Meg.

'Can you think of any other? Anyway, the point I was trying to make was that it would explain her getting rather more than friendly with Tengrala, in order to get hold of his key. She could then pass it on to Harte and everything would be satisfactory from their point of view.'

'That seems as good a solution as any other. The thing is, how to prove it.'

'Do you think Lieutenant Hennessey might help?'

'It's a possibility.' He paused as Jenny made a sudden uncharacteristically restless movement. 'Has something occurred to you, love?'

'I think you ought to see the others,' said Jenny. 'Tengrala's other friends. You see, it occurred to me – '

'Go on.'

'Well, this Margaret Charron, whom neither Meg nor I think sounds very nice ... if there are two men who are her lovers, why shouldn't there be a third?'

II

Only one other event enlivened the day to which they had been looking forward so much and which now found them all in subdued spirits. One thing, that is, besides dinner which set out to be deliberately festive, and left them more depressed than ever. It was a call from Washington, and Sir Huntley himself was on the line when Antony picked up the telephone. His first question was an anxious one. 'Are you all safe?'

'Perfectly safe, thank you, sir.'

'I'm afraid Jenny and your friend's wife must be upset.'

'Naturally so. If you're thinking they want us to leave the matter alone though – '

'Don't they?'

Antony smiled at the eager note in the older man's voice. 'As a matter of fact, no,' he said, 'but that may be because they realise it would be no use. I don't know whether you want me to continue or not, sir, but I'm going to find out who's responsible. I still see red every time I think of what might have happened.'

'I don't blame you for that, Antony. What precautions have you taken for your future safety?'

'Moved rooms, and instructed the switchboard not to give the new numbers to anyone.'

'That explains it then. They were quite willing to put me through, but not to tell me exactly where you were. Do you think that will answer?'

'I think so, sir.'

'Well, as far as I'm concerned I should like you to continue, more than ever since I received the information you conveyed to me so guardedly the other day.'

'I must admit, sir,' said Antony a trifle ruefully, 'that I didn't think of the explanation for your enthusiasm for myself. By my friend Farrell explained it to me. I believe that members of the Stock Exchange are sometimes more sophisticated than we of the law.'

'I said you weren't a diplomat,' said Sir Huntley triumphantly. 'When shall I see you again?'

'When I'm ready to make a full report. I don't see any point in coming down to Washington again until then.'

'That sounds sensible, but in the meantime you'll take care.' That was very much in the nature of an order and Antony agreed without argument. He thought as he rang off that Christmas Day 1973 was one he would never forget, and that he would remember it with no pleasure at all.

Wednesday, 26th December

I

After the before-Christmas bustle the city seemed strangely quiet as Antony and Roger made their way back to the Village the next morning, having completed certain tedious manoeuvres to ensure that any of Lieutenant Hennessey's minions who might be taking an interest in their movements did not accompany them. Not too early, not too late, Antony hoped. On the one hand there was the question of possible hangovers to consider; on the other, if they left it too late their quarry might have dispersed.

And that, in part, was what had happened, though the door did open this time to their knocking. Hanging on to the knob as though it were a lifeline was a small dark girl with an anxious look and a tea towel in her hand. The room immediately behind her was frankly a mess, there were sticky glasses and ashtrays unemptied, but it seemed she had started out on the long road to getting it tidy again.

'Are you Miss Crashaw?' Antony asked.

'Noella Crashaw, yes, I am.'

'I hope we haven't called at an inconvenient time,' Maitland went on, not altogether sincerely, the feelings of

Tengrala's associates being the last thing he was considering just then. 'We were hoping for a word with you, and with some of your friends whom I understand have lodgings here.'

Her chin went up. 'Jean and I live together,' she said with dignity. But obviously she was embarrassed by the admission, as Margaret Charron would never have been. 'The other two, Michael and Friedrich, they use the other bedroom.'

'May we come in?'

'Why, yes, I suppose so.' The suggestion obviously flustered her. 'But I'm all alone, the others went out.' She was backing away as she spoke and there was a wary look in her eyes as Roger followed Antony into the room and closed the door, shutting out the outside world. 'Do sit down. I'd like to get things cleared away first if you don't mind, just into the kitchen. I'll leave the dishes until later.'

'Perhaps we can help you,' said Roger. After all these years his unexpected streak of domesticity could still surprise his friend. Noella made a helpless gesture and without waiting for any further invitation he disappeared into what was presumably the kitchen, emerging a moment later with a large tray, on which he began expertly to pack the offending objects. Antony watched him, torn between amusement and a small feeling of envy. It was years now since he had carried a tray, the last time having ended ignominiously in tragedy to six Waterford sherry glasses of which Jenny was particularly fond, and though in general something as light as that was well within his capacity without strain to his shoulder he hadn't chanced it since.

'There!' said Roger, coming back with a satisfied air. The room, though still dusty and incredibly shabby, was no longer littered with the debris of last night's festivities. 'Won't you sit down, Miss Crashaw,' he added, rather as though he was in his own home instead of hers. 'Then my friend can tell you what we want of you.'

She obeyed gingerly, still with her eyes on Roger's face. 'You haven't told me your names,' she said.

'No, I'm sorry. That should have come first, shouldn't it? I'm Roger Farrell and this is my friend and colleague, Antony Maitland.'

She acknowledged the introduction with the merest inclination of her head, but her question was addressed again to Roger. 'What do you want?' she asked.

Roger glanced briefly at Maitland, but saw him relaxed and apparently quite willing to relinquish all share in the interview. He launched therefore into their agreed explanation. 'Poor Tengrala,' said Noella softly when he had finished. 'As if he would do a thing like that.'

'The evidence – ' said Roger, and paused as artistically as Antony himself might have done.

'I don't care about that, he wouldn't have done such a thing.'

Perhaps it was as well that Maitland was for the moment on the sidelines. He had heard that sentiment far too often from friends of one of his clients or another to bear with it patiently. 'Both the car and the weapon were traced to Mr Nema,' Roger went on. 'If he didn't use them himself, someone else did.'

'Yes, of course.'

'Somebody who knew the rifle was to be found in his flat, and who obtained access without leaving any traces of his presence, presumably by using a key.'

'Yes, but – '

'Tengrala Nema tells us he has very few friends in New York.'

'I know. Joel calls it keeping a low profile. But that *was* done, Mr – '

'Farrell,' Roger supplied.

'Yes, Mr Farrell. So it must have been possible. But not by one of us. We're his friends,' she insisted, 'and besides none of us has a key to his apartment, let alone to the building where he lives.'

'Can you be quite sure about that, Miss Crashaw?'

'Yes, I think so. When we've been over there Jean has always phoned first, and Tengrala has let us in himself.'

'Your friend Miss Charron had keys, 'said Antony suddenly from the depths of his chair. 'She told us that herself.'

His sudden incursion into the conversation seemed to startle her unduly, but she was in no doubt about her reply. 'Oh no, that's not possible,' she said quite firmly. 'Margaret and Joel, they belong together. In fact,' she said confidentially, 'I shouldn't be surprised if they got married one of these days. Jean says marriage is quite out of date – '

'A bourgeois concept,' Antony suggested, smiling.

'Yes, how did you know?'

'Something Tengrala said,' said Antony vaguely. 'This business of the keys, Miss Crashaw, Mr Farrell will confirm for you what Miss Charron told us about them.'

'Did she really?' She turned to Roger as she spoke.

'Yes, really,' he assured her. 'And the question is, you see, if she gave them to one of your other friends, who would that man have been?'

'Joel, but ... no, I don't believe that either.'

'One of the others might have thought up some excuse for needing them, and she might have handed them over quite innocently.'

'In that case, wouldn't she have told you?' she flashed back

124

at him. ' No, if she gave them to somebody it was to someone she was in love with, and that leaves only Joel.'

'We don't want to distress you, Miss Crashaw,' said Roger soothingly. 'Tengrala Nema has given us a certain explanation of the number of rifles found in his flat. I wonder if you could confirm that for us.'

That made her look doubtful all over again. 'I don't know if I should tell you,' she said. 'It was perfectly reasonable for him to have them, believe me, but I couldn't get up in court and tell you why.'

'This is for our own information only,' Antony put in. 'You know Tengrala and believe in him – '

'I believe in Joel too!'

' – but we met him for the first time the other day.'

'Well, it was just to help those poor people in Bosegwane. That's all any of us wanted.'

'If it came to the point,' said Antony, 'would you condone terrorist action to gain your ends?'

'No, of course not. Not on any account.'

'I wonder if you could speak so positively for your three friends.'

'They're all soldiers, Mr Maitland, and sometimes I think men don't see these things quite as we do.' (Speak for yourself, Antony thought, with Margaret Charron very vividly in his mind.) 'But I'm sure that none of them ... why should they shoot this Peter Ngala anyway, any more than Tengrala would?'

'I can think of reasons.' Maitland was vague again. 'Have you seen your friends, Joel Harte and Margaret Charron, since Christmas Eve?' he asked.

'No.'

'Have any of your friends seen them? Jean le Bovier for instance?'

'I'm sure he'd have told me if he had, but of course none of them are home all the time, as you can see for yourself.' And just at that moment, as though to confirm what she was saying, the door opened and a small, dapper man was framed in the entrance for a moment before he came in and closed the door sharply behind him.

'What's all this, Noella?' he said.

'Oh, Jean!' The look she gave him was one of pure adoration. 'It's about poor Tengrala. I think these gentlemen want to help him.'

'To do what? To escape justice?' His eyes moved for a moment questioningly from Maitland to Farrell. 'If you have the facilities, get him out of the country at once before the police make their move,' he advised. 'That's all you can do for him.'

Noella gave a kind of moan but she didn't attempt to contradict his statement.

'Monsieur le Bovier?' Antony asked. It was already obvious that Sir Huntley's vague reference to his skill in foreign languages being useful was not going to apply here. Unless, of course . . .

'I am he,' the newcomer claimed without hesitation.

'You're telling me that you believe Tengrala Nema to be guilty of shooting Peter Ngala?'

'Who else? But now I am thinking of it I believe I will not tell you anything more, until *you* have explained to *me* the reason for your questions. Noella, *ma chérie*, if our conversation disturbs you I'm sure there are things to be done . . . in the kitchen, say. Your birthday party seems to have left our quarters slightly dishevelled.'

'Yes, I'd like to finish clearing up. If you'll excuse me,' she added and again it was to Roger that the remark was addressed. She paused in the doorway, before going through to the kitchen and shutting herself in, to say over her shoulder, 'They've been very kind, Jean, and I'm sure they only mean to help Tengrala, not to harm the cause in any way.'

Jean le Bovier turned back to the two visitors, and suddenly the sharpness was gone both from his voice and his look. 'Noella forgot to introduce us,' he said.

This time Antony, as was usual, took the lead, effecting the introductions briefly. 'And now the explanation,' said le Bovier, 'and may it be a good one.'

'Do you mind telling me if you've seen either Joel Harte or Margaret Charron since Christmas Eve?'

'What a peculiar question.' He thought for a moment and then added slowly, 'I can't really see any harm in it. No, I haven't seen either of them.'

'And they didn't telephone you here?'

'No.'

'I was hoping, you see,' said Antony ingenuously, 'that one of them might have told you already, and so saved me the trouble of repeating myself. I find explanations so boring, don't you?'

'But necessary,' le Bovier insisted.

'Oh yes, indeed.' He embarked upon the familiar recital.

'I've told you you're wasting your time,' said le Bovier when he had finished. 'And I've told you why.'

'Because you believe Tengrala is guilty? Why are you so sure? I thought he was a friend of yours.'

'But certainly,' Jean shrugged.

'Miss Crashaw believes in his innocence.'

'Miss Crashaw is a sentimental little idiot. Don't misunderstand me, I should like to believe as she does. Tengrala after all is my . . . I've heard the phrase "my meal ticket" used, and it seems to me very apt.'

'I see.'

'I thought you would. Do I understand that Tengrala has confided in you?'

'To a certain extent, yes. To tell you the truth I'm not quite sure how far his confidences went.'

'And as the police have not been here, do I take it also that you have kept what he told you to yourselves?'

'We have. I advised him to tell his lawyer though.'

Le Bovier laughed. 'That would make a nice defence, would it not? The reason for the collection of rifles.'

'At least you can confirm that what Tengrala told me is true.'

'Did you doubt it? But as for the rest – '

'The murder of Peter Ngala you mean.'

'Yes. The facts are obvious, I think.'

'Can you suggest any motive?'

'I know something of both countries, Mr Maitland. Tim-kounou and Bosegwane. The emnity between them is not a secret. Shall I tell you my theory?'

'If you would be so good.'

'It is from the kindness of my heart you understand, so that you will not go on and make a fool of yourself over this matter. I have come to believe that the enmity between Louga Nema and Tengrala is a myth, that Tengrala carried out the murder at his father's instigation.'

'I see. Who drove the car, Monsieur le Bovier?'

'The car? How should I know a thing like that?'

'Tengrala has assured me that his acquaintance in New York is very slight, confined to you and your co-tenants of this apartment in fact, with the addition of a Mr Harte

128

and a Miss Charron.'

'*Ne sois pas bête.*'

Maitland looked at him blankly. 'I mean,' Jean elaborated, 'that because we are sympathetic with Tengrala in the enterprise of which he has spoken to us, a request for help in the matter of Peter Ngala's death would have given the game away, would have told us that his cover story was a myth. That is how you put it, is it not?'

'Yes, and I think I should congratulate you on your command of my language. There still remains the question, if your theory is right, who drove the car?'

'It makes no matter. One of the embassy staff *peutêtre.*'

'At least, m'sieur there is a certain consistency about the theory. Will you forgive me if I tell you that I don't believe a word of it.'

'*N'importe.*' Jean shrugged. '*Je sais que j'ai raison. Ça suffit.*'

'Of course,' said Maitland, vague again. 'When did you last see Tengrala?'

'Not long after the shooting.'

'Did you then think of him as a man who had recently committed murder?'

'I can believe many things of Tengrala, but not that he is a coward. He would think no more of such an act than of – of crushing a beetle. The use of the word "murder" is inappropriate.'

'I understand you used to meet at his apartment. But you say that only once since Peter Ngala's death – '

'On the second occasion that we went there it was only too obvious that the place was under police supervision. I warned my friends and we came away.'

'Who was with you on that occasion?'

'Noella, of course. And our friends who share our lodgings.

129

Michael O'Shaughnessy and Friedrich Schiller.' On the whole, Tengrala had made a better attempt at the Irishman's name than le Bovier did.

'Did you phone Tengrala to tell him why the meeting did not take place? I suppose he was expecting you.'

'No, I didn't warn him. Who was to say that someone could not have been listening in? But I did phone Joel Harte to say that he and Margaret should stay away.'

'How did you and your two friends come to be mixed up in this business?'

'We'd been comrades in arms before. We were sent here . . . no that's something I think I shall not tell you, Mr Maitland . . . who sent us here. Later Tengrala came and was told to get in touch with us.'

'You made a convert of Miss Crashaw,' said Roger suddenly.

Jean turned to him with a smile. 'An appealing little thing, is she not? A convert? Yes, perhaps. But if I tell her black is white she will believe it, which makes me doubt her real attachment to the cause.'

'Miss Charron?' Antony hazarded.

'Ah, there you have a woman. *Elle fait ses quatre volontés.* What I am saying is that she knows her own mind.'

'Thank you. You've been very kind, Monsieur le Bovier, to give us so much of your time.'

'And in being so open with you,' Jean added. 'Doesn't that surprise you?'

'No. Tengrala was also frank with us, and as we know so much it can do little harm to tell us more. Besides,' he paused to smile at the Frenchman, 'I'm sure it has occurred to you, as it occurred I believe to Mr Harte and Miss Charron, that I'm less likely to speak of your plans to the wrong people if you co-operate with me.'

'That is very acute of you. It had occurred to me too.'

'Then, since we are so far in agreement, may I ask you to take your kindness one step further? Assume for a moment that Tengrala Nema did not shoot Peter Ngala.'

'What then?'

'In that case his car was stolen and a rifle from his apartment borrowed. This could only have been done by someone who knew about the rifles and who could recognise his car. The first point is the material one. Add that this person must also have been able to get into the apartment without leaving any trace of forcible entry. That being so we must suppose he had keys. So I'm asking you whether you or any of your companions has ever had the keys to that apartment and, of course, to the building in his possession.'

'Most certainly not. Why should we?'

Maitland ignored that. 'Miss Charron has admitted to us that she had, and I suppose still has, the keys.'

That brought a quick frown. 'She told you? Just like that?'

'She could hardly do anything else, since Tengrala had already informed us of the fact.'

'*Foutaise*! But why should he have given her them I wonder.'

'For obvious reasons I should think, which she made no attempt to deny to us. After all, in today's permissive society – '

'*Mais un moricaud*!'

'I'm not quite sure ... do I understand you don't altogether approve of the association, Monsieur le Bovier?'

'It's no affair of mine,' said Jean quickly. 'But there are things ... Yes, Mr Maitland, I am not yet beyond being surprised.'

'Then, still assuming Tengrala's innocence, to whom do

131

you think she would have given these keys?'

'If you are right, I imagine she kept them strictly for her own use, and not for the purpose of extracting a rifle or the car keys. I don't think I like this game we're playing, Mr Maitland. I am not an imaginative man.'

'You don't think that as she lives with Mr Harte – '

'Yes, of course, it would have to be to him. But I don't agree with the idea on which you base your theory. I must make that quite clear.'

'I don't think you left us in any doubt as to your opinion. Monsieur le Bovier, you are an intelligent man. How devoted are you to "the cause", as Miss Crashaw calls it?'

'I am a realist, Mr Maitland. Our friend, Tengrala, *il perdre son temps*. When I dedicate myself to any cause it will be one worthy of my respect, and with some prospect of lasting gain. But the petty affairs of a petty African state . . .' for a moment his sincerity had been obvious, but now he seemed to recollect himself. 'It is as I have said, a matter of money.'

Antony got to his feet and Roger followed suit with some alacrity. 'Can you add to your kindness by telling us where we would be likely to find your friends Mr O'Shaughnessy and Mr Schiller?'

'Michael you'll very likely find in the bar at the end of the street, *The Golden Fleece*. And if you're going to say it's rather early for drinking, Mr Maitland, let me tell you you don't know Mike. He has a hard head, but also *tête d'épingle*.' He laughed shortly, seeing Maitland's expression of bewilderment. 'As for Friedrich, I can only say, *Dingue*, and I'm afraid I don't know where he might be.'

'We'll try *The Golden Fleece* then. Thank you very much, Monsieur le Bovier, and will you convey our thanks to Miss Crashaw as well?'

He was going towards the door when the telephone rang sharply. Crossing the room with the obvious intention of seeing them off the premises, Jean was just beside it and snatched it up before it could ring again. '*Ah, c'est toi, chérie,*' he said after listening for a moment. '*Où pouvons-nous nous rencontrer?*' He listened again for a moment. '*Bien,*' he said at last. '*Et dans l'intervalle, faites attention à ce que vous dites.*' He put down the receiver and turned, smiling, to bid his guests adieu. 'It has been a great pleasure,' he told them. 'I only wish there were more things on which we could agree.'

II

'Well, what did you think of that?' said Roger as they went out into the street again. Fortunately, as it turned out, they hadn't asked the cab to wait. 'Do we go down to this *Golden Fleece* place and try to confront Michael O'Shaughnessy there?'

'Oh yes, I think so. It seems as good an idea as any.'

Roger fell into step beside him. 'What did you think of le Bovier's theory?' he asked.

'Which theory was that?'

'About Tengrala's motive.'

'Not much. If we were to believe him, Tengrala Nema went through an elaborate and rather expensive charade to hide his real intentions. Besides, I think Louga Nema is genuinely hurt by his son's attitude, which he wouldn't be if they were in cahoots.'

'What did le Bovier say when you implied to him that Margaret Charron had been carrying on with Tengrala? I got some of the rest of it, but that went past too quickly.'

'You won't find it in the dictionary, at least I'd be surprised if you did. I don't know whether it's translatable . . . nonsense, perhaps. And he does not admire the mental accomplishments of his two comrades-in-arms, in fact, he doesn't seem to have a good word for anybody, except the ladies. Talking of which, he's conventional enough not to like a white girl carrying on with a negro, or a blackamoor as he put it. But then, how many of us live up to our convictions all the time?'

By this time they had reached the end of the street, and were confronted by a shabby door with half obliterated lettering. 'That might say *The Golden Fleece*, but then again, it might not,' said Antony. 'However, let's try.'

It was dark inside. ('But even in the best regulated places,' said Antony later to Meg and Jenny, 'New Yorkers seem to think there's something shameful about being seen having a drink.') However, when their eyes became accustomed to the gloom they saw a big room with a bar along the far end, and a number of tables scattered about, each with its quota of four anything-but-easy chairs. Roger, whose nature it was to see everything in simple terms, was already making his way to the bar. 'Is this *The Golden Fleece*?' he demanded.

'Yes, it is. What about it?'

'We couldn't quite read the notice outside,' said Antony, coming up apologetically to his friend's side, 'but we're looking for a Mr Michael O'Shaughnessy and we understand he may be here.'

'Mike? What do you want with Mike?' But the barman's eyes went involuntarily to a table in the far corner, and Maitland felt himself released from the problem of replying.

'Over there is he? Thank you so much.' Deliberately provocative, as Roger complained later, but at the moment it had the desired effect of silencing the man behind the bar. 'Perhaps we could have a couple of beers. Would you mind waiting for them, Roger?'

'Imported?' said the barman sourly.

'That would be splendid.' He was already on his way across the room, and he thought as he drew near the table that if he had taken the trouble to look around him a little longer he would have known his quarry anywhere, a big man, though without an ounce of fat on him, with curly black hair and an open, cheerful expression. The only trouble was, he wasn't alone. But at least none of the tables nearby was occupied.

'Mr O'Shaughnessy?'

The big man nodded, apparently not at all put out or surprised at being so addressed by a stranger. 'We've just come from your lodgings, and they said we might find you here. My friend and I want a word with you, do you mind if we join you? Perhaps you'd let us buy you a drink.'

'You may be sure of that. Same again, Eddie,' he called down the room to the barman. There was a faintest touch of brogue in his accent, though time or his travels seemed to have altered what might have been his natural way of wording things. But that was something that didn't occur to Antony until later. At the moment his only thought was that, like Lieutenant Hennessey, this new acquaintance was not above assuming a manner of speech not completely natural to him.

'And what might you be after wanting with me?' asked O'Shaughnessy as Roger approached with a tray.

'A word or two in private. My name is Maitland, and this is my friend, Roger Farrell.'

'Private is it? There's nothing you can say to me I wouldn't want my friend Fred to hear.'

That riveted Antony's attention more closely for a moment on the second man. Much smaller than his companion, with rather lank fair hair that looked as if it would have been none the worse for a wash. There was besides far too much of it. 'I wonder,' said Maitland tentatively, 'if by any chance this is Mr Friedrich Schiller.'

'That's right. And who might you be?'

'In that case, it's both of you we want to see. Good morning, Herr Schiller.' Fred maintained his silence, and Maitland embarked once again on his bowdlerised explanation.

'And how did you come to connect us with this Tengrala Nema's affairs?' said O'Shaughnessy rather belligerently when he had finished.

'I understand you're friends of his.'

'That isn't quite good enough.'

'But perhaps when I've gone a little further you'll find it so. You know, of course, of the police suspicions of Tengrala in respect of the murder of Peter Ngala?'

'He told us of them himself the one time I've seen him since that unhappy event.' All hint of brogue had vanished now.

'What do you think about them?'

'Shall I be frank with you?'

Antony smiled at him. 'I imagine you will be, whatever I say.'

'All right then. He wouldn't have the guts to do a thing like that.'

'And yet he is engaged, I understand, in an operation not far short of terrorism?'

'Did he tell you that?'

'He did, to explain the reason the rifles were found in his apartment.'

'Well, you've got the terrorism bit wrong. Tengrala is a romantic.'

'Is he though?' said Antony, contemplating this new idea

136

with surprise.

'Revolution yes, terrorism no,' said Michael emphatically.

'Are those your sentiments too, Mr O'Shaughnessy?'

'I do what I'm paid for, no more, no less. The rights and wrongs of the situation don't concern me.'

'I see. Then you can confirm Tengrala's explanation for the rifles.'

'What do you mean to do about it?'

'I've advised him to tell his lawyer, beyond that I shall do nothing. To put it in legal terms, Mr O'Shaughnessy, it is not a matter about which I know anything of my own knowledge.'

'In that case, all right. He was telling you the truth.'

'Have you seen him recently?'

'Only the once since Peter Ngala's death. We went together – you've been talking to Jean and Noella, so you know who I mean – but Jean must have had his suspicions that somebody might be watching the apartment, he wouldn't let us go in, and we've none of us been there since.'

'There were two other people who knew of this – may I say conspiracy? – of yours.'

'You may call it what you like so long as you keep your mouth shut about it.'

'That's doesn't answer my question.'

'No. However, I've no real objection to doing so. Their names are Margaret Charron and Joel Harte, and they live together as Jean and Noella do.'

'Have you seen either of them since Christmas Eve, say?'

'Why Christmas Eve?'

'That doesn't matter, but I should like an answer to my question.'

'Oh, very well! No, I haven't seen either of them.'

'Are they both with you in this heart and soul?'

'Margaret is. But she's another romantic, just such another as Tengrala. Joel? I think we can trust him, she says we can, but he isn't really part of the ... conspiracy was your word, wasn't it, Mr Maitland? He only knows about it because of his association with Margaret.'

'That brings me to the most important question of all. You believe Tengrala to be innocent?'

'I've said so.'

'The corollary won't have escaped you, but in that case someone else is guilty.'

'Peter Ngala may have had many enemies.'

'Come now, Mr O'Shaughnessy, you're not so naive as that.' Michael picked up his glass and disposed of the contents, which Antony suspected had been neat whisky, at a gulp.

'The hair of the dog,' he said amiably. 'Last night was quite a night. Will your funds run to another?'

'I think it might be arranged.' Again there was a call down the length of the room to the barman, who this time brought the drinks himself.

'I suppose you mean,' said Michael O'Shaughnessy after the man had gone, 'that whoever killed Ngala had access to Tengrala's apartment, and knew at least that the rifles would be there. The car keys might have been a bonus.'

'That's exactly what I do mean,' Maitland agreed.

'And there were no signs of forcible entry?'

"It seems obvious that a key was used, to effect entrance to the building as well as to the apartment itself.'

'Then I can't help you.'

'I think perhaps you may be able to. Tengrala tells me that one set of keys to his apartment is in the possession of Mar-

138

garet Charron.'

'The devil!' said Michael. It was difficult to believe that he was not genuinely surprised.

'So the question arises – '

'What does Joel have to say to that?'

'He doesn't know. You're in no doubt then, Mr O'Shaughnessy, any more than I am, of the reason Tengrala gave her the key.'

'It's no business of mine. If she wants to play fast and loose with Joel – '

'That doesn't concern me either. What I am interested in though is to whom she might have given or lent the keys.'

'I don't like this,' said Michael uneasily. 'I don't like it at all. Is Tengrala quite sure – '

'Quite sure that no-one else has the keys. Yes, he says so.'

'Then I can only think . . . Joel. And it might be that he knew what was happening and condoned it because he wanted to gain possession of the keys. But that seems to me almost as unlikely as Tengrala's guilt.'

'It has been pointed out to me that a woman who has – shall we say – two strings to her bow may well have a third.'

'Not guilty. I prefer something a little more, a little more yielding. Now if Noella weren't head-over-heels in love with Jean – '

'Yes, I take your point. The other members of your circle though – '

'Jean and Fred here? What do you think of that, Fred old boy? Have you been carrying on with Margaret?'

'*Konnten Sie etwas langsamer sprechen?*'

'Eh?' O'Shaughnessey was obviously completely taken aback.

'He asked you,' said Maitland, very slowly indeed, 'if by

139

any chance you had had an affair with Margaret Charron.'
Friedrich Schiller shook his head dumbly.

'*Lass uns vernuftig sein. Ich verstehe Sie.* We can quite well
conduct our conversation in your own language if you prefer,'
Antony went on reasonably.

Schiller scowled at him. 'It has not been my experience
that your compatriots have much facility in languages other
than their own,' he said.

'It just shows you should never take anything for granted.
What about answering our friend Mr O'Shaughnessy's questions?'

'About Margaret Charron?' Oddly, Schiller sounded
amused. 'An attractive woman,' he said. 'Not for me.'

'I take it, *mein Herr*, you're not going to deny having understood our conversation with your friend.' Schiller, who
seemed to be a man of as few words as possible, inclined his
head. Maitland was finding it increasingly difficult to think
of him as Fred. Friedrich perhaps, but on the whole more
formality seemed appropriate, whereas for the cheerful Irishman, Michael, the diminutive of Mike came naturally to
mind. 'You'll know then why I'm asking you these questions,
and that your friend Tengrala has to some extent confided in
me. So I must ask you whether you can think of anyone,
besides Mr Harte, with whom Miss Charron might be
intimate.'

'We have all been good friends.'

'That wasn't what I meant, as I think you know. Perhaps
you don't want to answer that question with your friend Mr
O'Shaughnessy here.' He caught Michael's eye as he spoke,
and detected a decided gleam of humour in it.

'No, it is not that at all,' said Schiller seriously. 'So far as he knows he has told you the truth. But on his own admission, Tengrala – '

'We are at the moment assuming Tengrala's innocence. Or have you any quarrel with that?'

'None at all. He is a boy in a man's world, useful to us only as a figurehead.'

'Or as someone to take the blame if your plans are discovered?'

'That I did not say. As to this question of intimacy,' – his tone poured scorn on the word – 'I cannot help you.'

'Do you think Miss Charron is sincerely dedicated to your cause?'

'As much as is in her. She is a woman and therefore light minded.'

'Like Noella Crashaw?'

'I see no difference between them.'

That doesn't say much for your powers of observation, Maitland thought. Aloud he said, 'What is your own opinion about the battle you're prepared to wage?'

Schiller shrugged. 'I am being paid, that is enough. Besides I have fought together with these two in the past – '

'With le Bovier and O'Shaughnessy?'

'That is what I meant. They are two men whom I trust in that respect.'

'Then you can confirm Tengrala's story about the reason for the rifles being in his apartment?'

'For your ears only, yes.'

'When did you see him last?'

'You have heard what Michael told you. It is true.'

'And have you seen either Joel Harte or Margaret Charron since Christmas Eve?'

'Again – '

141

'No, Herr Schiller, this time I should like you to speak for yourself.'

'Very well. I have not seen either of them since then.'

'Do you feel Mr Harte is a dedicated member of your conspiracy?'

'I do not like the word, and I think he is a sentimental fool who will believe what Margaret tells him.'

'I see. What were you trying to hide, Herr Schiller, when you pretended not to understand me?'

'It is only that I do not like answering questions,' Schiller explained. A sentiment with which Maitland concurred so completely that he hadn't the heart to press the matter further. In any case, he thought he knew . . .

'In that case, gentlemen, we must thank you and leave you,' he said, pushing his chair back and getting to his feet. 'Purely as a matter of curiosity, however, how are you placed for funds since you haven't been in touch with Tengrala?'

Schiller frowned over that, but O'Shaughnessy answered in his expansive way. 'Are you concerned for our welfare, Mr Maitland? That's good of you, but we're well supplied.'

'Then may I give you a piece of advice? As I have told you, I don't consider your doings any direct concern of mine, nor am I familiar with the United States law on gun running. But you are intelligent men, you two and Mr le Bovier, and there are other occupations open to you, I'm sure, besides that of mercenaries. Not so well paid perhaps, but more long lived.' Having said which he divided a smile impartially between them and turned on his heel. Roger wasn't far behind him.

III

When they got back to the hotel Antony glanced into the

dining-room before they went upstairs. 'No sign of Jenny,' he reported, 'but there was rather a crowd in there, I don't think we could talk. Shall we have lunch sent upstairs?'

'You aren't usually so ready to face a barrage of questions,' said Roger following him towards the elevator. 'Which is exactly what you'll get, particularly if Meg has got back.'

'That can't be helped. Anyway it was part of the deal to be open with them. But actually I'm afraid I'm more prompted by a desire to clear my head than to provide enlightenment.'

As it happened, Meg had got back from the theatre, and was waiting with Jenny in the Maitlands' room. 'Half the cast didn't turn up, darlings,' she complained as soon as she saw them, 'but as I told Ossie it was only to be expected over the holiday.'

'How many times have I to remind you that you're not working for Ossie over here?' said Roger, making for the table where the telephone stood and picking up the room service menu which was beside the instrument.

'But, Roger darling, they're so alike. And I don't see how anybody could expect ... but that doesn't matter now. Here I am, and Jenny and I are both agog to hear what you've been doing.'

'At the present moment,' said Roger, 'I'm ordering drinks for us all and a little nourishment.' He broke off and began to speak into the telephone. 'And don't tell me you couldn't care less if you never saw another turkey,' he added a moment later, laying down the receiver, 'because turkey hash is what you're getting.'

'Don't tell me that was on the menu,' said Meg.

'Not exactly, but the voice at the other end was recommending it as the Chef's Special, so I thought we'd better take a chance. And if Antony has anything to tell you,' he added, seating himself on the dressing-table stool and swirling round to face them, 'it's more than I have. I couldn't make head nor tail of what was being said, except that his questions must have put the cat among the pigeons.'

'Nonsense, I was discretion itself,' said Antony, rather amused by his friend's vehemence.

'Did you manage to see all the people you wanted to see?' asked Jenny.

'Yes, we did. Starting with Noella Crashaw, going on to Jean le Bovier . . . both those interviews were conducted at the apartment they occupy. And then we went to talk to Michael O'Shaughnessy at a nearby bar, and were lucky enough to find Friedrich Schiller with him.'

'In that case they must have told you *something*,' Jenny objected. 'I can't believe it was a pure waste of time, Roger.'

'Probably not, from Antony's point of view,' Roger admitted. 'I always said he could see further through a brick wall than most people. But he's the one with the memory who's used to preparing reports. Let him tell you himself.'

'Darling, that's what we're waiting for,' said Meg.

As Maitland had said, there were things he wanted to get clear in his own mind, and this was a good opportunity. Even so, so far as facts were concerned, the telling didn't take very long. The end of his narrative coincided with the arrival of the drinks and their lunch, and by common consent they tackled that important matter first. When they had finished Jenny stacked everything tidily and Roger pushed the table out of the way, so that there was nothing left to distract them.

'All right, Antony,' he said. 'Jenny and Meg know as much as we do now. The question is, what do you make of it all?'

'This and that.' His eyes went from one to the other of his companions. 'Any bright ideas?' he asked.

144

'Joel Harte still seems to be the most likely person for Margaret Charron to have given the key to,' said Jenny, rather hesitantly because she didn't like the idea of condemning anybody.

But Meg had her own ideas. 'Don't you think it was rather suspicious,' she suggested, 'that this man, Schiller, pretended he couldn't speak English?'

'I think he was telling the truth when he said he didn't like answering questions. I have an idea about that – '

'Of course you have,' said Meg resignedly.

Roger seemed to have been following his own train of thought, and he interrupted at this point. 'Noella Crashaw is in it for love,' he said, 'that's very obvious. As for the other three, the mercenaries, they none of them seem particularly dedicated to the cause of Bosegwane's freedom, but in the circumstances I think that's natural.'

'All the same – ' Antony began.

'I knew you'd got somewhere,' said Jenny triumphantly. 'Are you going to tell us?'

'It's not really conclusive, nothing like proof,' her husband warned her. 'Just a few points that occurred to me.'

'Tell us!' Meg demanded imperiously.

'It began with Jenny's suggestion that if Margaret Charron had two lovers she might well have a third.'

'Thereby lessening the odds against Joel Harte,' said Meg, nodding.

'Precisely.' He paused a moment, because that was a remark that generally brought a wail from Meg that he was getting exactly like Uncle Nick, but on this occasion she was too absorbed in the problem. 'Following on that there were two other points: Margaret Charron and Jean le Bovier were the only two of the six who felt – or said they felt – that there was no doubt about Tengrala's guilt. Did you think he was really in love with Noella, Roger?' he demanded, turning suddenly to Farrell.

'No, I didn't. I thought it was a pretty one-sided affair. And he did seem to admire Margaret Charron,' Roger added rather doubtfully.

'He did, and he went a step further. He was definitely upset when I implied pretty strongly that she was having an affair with Tengrala as well as with Joel Harte.'

'Was that what you were aiming for?' asked Roger. 'His reaction? I noticed you played him differently from the way you treated Schiller, not letting on that you understood what he was saying for instance.'

'Well, you must admit it was illuminating, because quite obviously Tengrala's colour made the idea more repugnant to him.'

'Wait a bit!' That was Meg, echoing a favourite exclamation of Maitland's. 'If you're deducing from all this that le Bovier set Margaret Charron on to getting the keys from Tengrala, none of this could have been a surprise to him.'

'Oh, but I think it could. I don't think he had the faintest idea that Tengrala knew she had the keys. I think she told Jean le Bovier some quite innocent story about how she got hold of them, but once he realised that Tengrala knew all about it ... well the cat was among the pigeons, as you said, Roger.'

'It certainly fits the facts, Antony,' said Roger slowly, 'the trouble is – '

'It isn't proof,' said Maitland.

'It seems to me to be a perfectly valid theory,' said Roger, laying a little stress on the final word. 'The trouble is, there are two others just as good.'

146

'Tell me,' said Antony, though less demandingly than Meg had done when she used almost the same words a moment before.

'All right, I will. One is the obvious one that Tengrala Nema is as guilty as the police think he is; that nobody had his keys – '

'Except Margaret Charron,' Maitland reminded him.

'But, if this happens to be true, she had them merely for the purpose of pleasure and not for any more sinister reason,' said Roger. 'Tengrala therefore used one of the rifles that were in his flat, and abandoned his car in case it had been recognised, so that the story of its being stolen shouldn't seem too far-fetched.'

'Who drove it?'

'How should I know? Perhaps le Bovier was right and some member of Louga Nema's staff took the wheel.'

'All right, that's one theory. What of the other?'

'Jenny's idea that Joel Harte committed the murder.'

'I only said he sounded the most likely,' said Jenny, a little distressed.

'Yes, love, I know you did,' said Antony comfortingly. 'And I have to agree with both you and Roger that it's perfectly possible. But there's still the third theory,' he added, turning to Farrell, 'the one I've just propounded to you, that Jean le Bovier and Margaret Charron were accomplices.'

'Is it any more likely than the other two?' asked Roger.

'I think it is. Somebody drove the car after all.'

'Couldn't she have done it for one of the others?'

'For Harte perhaps. I don't think for Tengrala. If his purposes were not the ones he disclosed to these co-conspirators of his, how would he have dared to admit that to her?'

'Doesn't that apply to the others?'

'No, because from what we hear she co-opted Harte into the conspiracy, not the other way round. Besides I don't think she's in love with him, any more than she's serious about Tengrala. But she may well have a crush on le Bovier. And there are other ways in which an extreme, though misguided, regard for human rights might manifest itself besides by taking part in a plot to liberate Bosegwane.'

'And what would *his* motive be?' Meg demanded.

'To bring about the very situation Sir Huntley Gorsford is afraid of, namely that Timkounou will invade Bosegwane, thereby giving the Communists an excuse to intervene. What do we know about le Bovier's real feelings, after all?'

'There's something he said,' said Roger slowly.

'Yes, I haven't forgotten. I was just about to bring that point up to clinch my argument. If I'm right about his feelings about Margaret Charron he'd just received the hell of a jolt when he heard of her affair with Tengrala, which is probably why he spoke so openly. He spoke of a cause worthy of respect and holding some prospect of lasting gain. As we all know, he wouldn't be the first person to apply that description to Communism.'

'That occurred to me too,' Roger admitted, 'especially when he seemed to recollect himself suddenly and change his course. But then I thought it might just be that he was ashamed, as some men are, of displaying any genuine emotion.'

'I've a couple of other points to make. One is that le Bovier was the one to prevent any further contact between his friends and Tengrala by saying his apartment was being watched by the police. We know that wasn't true.'

'We might not have noticed,' said Roger.

'I should,' Antony told him positively.

'All right, but – '

'There was something about why Mr Schiller didn't want to talk to you,' Jenny reminded her husband.

'I was just coming to that, love. I think he knew, or guessed, that there was something – good God, how mealy-mouthed can you get? – between Jean le Bovier and Margaret Charron.'

'How do you make that out?' asked Roger curiously.

'He said, about his friend Mike, that he had told us the truth about Miss Charron *so far as he knows it*. And he qualified his statement that he could trust his two companions-in-arms by adding *in that respect*, meaning, I took it, in fighting. If he had some inkling of le Bovier's true feelings ...'

'I think you've made your point,' said Roger seriously.

'Thank you. I should also like to add that to me at least my impressions of Tengrala and of Joel Harte carry a good deal of weight. One of them might be a disguised Communist, but I don't think either of them is a murderer.'

'And that,' said Meg, suddenly stretching out a hand and patting her husband, 'as we very well know, Roger darling, is probably as good as argument as any. Not that I don't agree with you, Antony, but the thing is, what are you going to do about it?'

'I should like to go to the police, but I shall have to get H.E.'s permission first.'

'Do you think he'll give it?'

'I don't see why not.'

'There's this business of disclosing the conspiracy,' said Roger. 'Tengrala's conspiracy I must call it, though I'm aware he has a leader whose name we don't know. I gather that neither Her Majesty's Government nor the State Department here are particularly keen on that being made public.'

'I thought you were going to remind me of my promise about that,' said Antony. 'I see no reason why I shouldn't propound my theory to Lieutenant Hennessey without mentioning that the six people we've been talking to are anything more than good friends of Tengrala's.'

'He won't believe you,' Roger asserted.

'He may not, but if I can raise enough doubt in his mind to make him look into the matter further ... you know what Chief Inspector Sykes always says, once you know where to look all kinds of things come to light. The police have facilities for that kind of thing, but we don't.'

That was so manifestly true that Roger made no further objection. 'Use the phone in our room if you want to talk to Sir Huntley alone,' he offered.

That seemed to Antony a good idea, and he availed himself of the invitation without delay. Coming back some fifteen minutes later he announced without preamble, 'He says okay, but he wants to see me first.'

'Does that mean you'll be away for two days again?' asked Jenny.

'No, our talk shouldn't take very long this time. I'll go up in the morning by train as I did before, and catch a late train back. Why don't you hire a car, Roger, then you can take Jenny sightseeing while Meg is at the theatre?'

That afternoon they walked in the park, and enjoyed their dinner all the better for it. It wasn't until the following morning at breakfast time that any of them realised that all their carefully laid plans had gone awry once again.

Thursday, 27th December

I

Most of the hotel's patrons at that time of the year had nothing on their minds but amusement, and it was not surprising, therefore, that the dining-room was almost deserted when they went down. Roger fell upon the newspaper as soon as they were seated and the waiter had poured their coffee. Meg pulled an apologetic face at her companions. 'You mustn't mind him, darlings, he's always like this at breakfast time.'

'Quite unreasonable,' said Antony solemnly, though Jenny could have told you that he wasn't above doing the same thing himself. 'There can't possibly be any financial news so soon after the holiday.'

'No, but there's something else,' said Roger.

'We're at war,' said Antony, rather more flippantly than he should have done.

'No, but I'm not at all sure you won't think it's almost as bad. Here, this paragraph at the bottom of the page.' He handed the paper to his friend and explained to Meg and Jenny as Antony read the item for himself. 'Margaret Charron was murdered late yesterday afternoon, and Joel Harte has been arrested.'

'Oh, my God,' said Antony, and his words were an intercession rather than an imprecation. 'This comes of my meddling, I suppose.'

Jenny was looking stricken, but Meg said bracingly, 'Nonsense, darling!' while Roger took on himself more explicitly the role of comforter.

'You'd already decided, hadn't you, that Margaret Charron was the accomplice, at least, of the person who murdered Peter Ngala, and that she probably drove the car herself? There's an old saying that those who live by the sword die by the sword, and even if you were wrong about Jean le Bovier being the man who fired the rifle, there's no harm done. She got no more than she deserved.'

'I wonder if she'd agree with you. But I don't think I was wrong.'

'What then? Did Harte find out after all that Margaret Charron was carrying on with Tengrala, and was this a simple crime of passion?'

'I don't think that for a moment either. I think it's the direct cause of our talking – I should say of my talking – to le Bovier. Do you remember how he reacted when he heard under what pretext she got the key of Tengrala's apartment? I certainly think jealousy comes into it, but I still think he was the guilty party, of this crime as well as of the other.'

'So what are you going to do?'

'Exactly what I proposed last night, only I shall do it today instead of tomorrow.'

'And Sir Huntley?'

'I'll phone him, of course, and tell him our meeting today is off.'

'He may not like it,' Jenny ventured, speaking for the first time since her husband had read the upsetting paragraph.

'I dare say he won't but that can't be helped. I'll go to Hennessey,' he decided. 'I know this particular murder won't be anything to do with him, but when I explain the connection with the one he *is* concerned with – '

'He may think Tengrala is guilty of both,' said Meg, in her most Cassandra-like tone.

'Don't be so encouraging, *darling*. I'll phone Sir Huntley now, while you order,' he added, getting to his feet. 'The usual for me. I don't suppose it will take long.'

He was wrong about that. Sir Huntley, surprised while he was shaving, was not in the best of tempers, and not at all inclined to agree to the course of action Maitland suggested without prior consultation. 'All right then, Antony,' he said at last, with an obvious attempt at being reasonable. 'You go to this Lieutenant Hennessey and he won't believe a word you say. Where will you be then?'

'In that case, sir, I shall take matters into my own hands and deal with them as I feel best.' Maitland's statement was perhaps a little more vehement than was courteous.

'Not without consulting me.'

'Yes, sir, without consulting you any further. If you'll forgive my saying so I don't find your attitude at the moment exactly helpful.'

'But how will this help Tengrala Nema?'

Antony's tone softened a little. 'Uncle Nick often accuses me of being single-minded,' he said. 'I think in this instance I could accuse you of the same thing, Your Excellency.'

'How do you mean?' asked Sir Huntley suspiciously.

'I mean that I think Joel Harte is innocent, and diplomacy or no diplomacy I don't intend to see him convicted of something he didn't do.'

'You always were stubborn, even as a boy,' said Sir

153

Huntley thoughtfully.

'Yes, sir, very probably. You do see my point though, don't you?'

'Yes, I understand. It accords with all I've heard of you. All the same, Antony,' his tone was milder now, 'if you insist on taking your own way I can't be held responsible – '

'I understand that, sir,' said Antony quickly. 'No diplomatic immunity, no connection with the Embassy at all in fact. That doesn't worry me, I'm not proposing to break the law.'

'I imagine obstructing the police is as unfavourably looked on here as it is at home.'

'I intend to help, not hinder.' Almost as though he was arguing with his uncle, the hint of opposition was raising Antony's spirits. 'Trust me, sir, I'll keep the Embassy out of it.'

'I seem to have no choice but to trust you.' There was the hint of grimness in Sir Huntley's voice again. 'All the same, Antony, you'll keep me advised. Don't, I implore you, don't do anything foolhardy.'

'I don't *think* I shall,' said Maitland doubtfully.

'What does that mean?'

'If Hennessey will listen to me, well and good. If not . . . you mustn't forget, sir, I have a score to settle with the joker who planted those bombs on Christmas Day.'

'I told you I was sorry about that.'

'Yes, that's not the p-point. Roger and I might be c-considered fair g-game, but when it comes to Jenny and Meg, not to mention the ch-chambermaids and the other people who might have been nearby in the hotel, that's altogether too m-much.'

'If you lose your temper,' His Excellency warned him, 'you

154

won't be in a state to deal with the situation.'

'No, that's r-right, sir. I'll do my best to keep it in ch-check. As for advising you, of course I will if you like. But I also warn you now that you may not like what you hear.'

'That's what I'm afraid of,' said Sir Huntley, and did not seem to be much comforted by the time they finished their conversation and rang off about five minutes later.

When Maitland got back to the dining-room he found Roger alone. 'Meg had to go,' he said, 'and Jenny went to cancel the car we'd ordered. I think she thought you might like to talk to me alone.'

'Well, it's just as she said, Sir Huntley didn't like what I proposed one little bit. I think he was coming round to my way of thinking in the end, though he couldn't give us his official blessing, of course, we're quite on our own from now on. But Hennessey is a good sort of chap, Roger. I don't think talking to him will be too difficult.'

'And if he won't listen,' said Roger just as Sir Huntley had done.

'That's a different matter. It will mean seeing our conspirators again, a job for one of us, not two.'

'By one of us I take it you mean yourself,' said Roger. 'Well, that's out. If anything is to come of it, you'll need a witness to what's said, and if there's any rough stuff you may find me useful.'

'You needn't remind me that this blasted shoulder makes me practically helpless,' said Antony with an edge to his tone. And then, immediately contrite, 'Sorry, Roger. There's no-one I'd rather have with me, but – '

'You're thinking that neither of us is equipped to stop a bullet.'

'Well, no, not exactly. If you want to know what I think,

it's that those particular rooms will be quite innocent of anything in the way of armaments. I know that's how they'd be
if I was one of the conspirators. Tengrala, after all, was willing
to take the responsibility for that kind of thing.'

'So you may need me,' said Roger triumphantly.

'I admit I'd prefer to have you along, but what I was
thinking about was Meg, and Jenny too.'

'Meg would never forgive me, and if you think I want to
live with your ghost standing between the two of us you're
very much mistaken,' Roger retorted. 'Besides the last thing
she said to me was, "If he wants to do anything silly make sure
you go along and see that he doesn't get altogether out of
hand." So you see – '

'I see she's as bad as Jenny, who'll never stand in the
way of anything I feel I ought to do,' said Antony. 'I wish
to goodness she wasn't at the theatre, though, it means
leaving Jenny alone. But for the moment we're only going
to tell her we're going to see Hennessey, she can't object
to that.'

If Roger thought that Jenny knew her husband well
enough by now to realise his probable further course of
action, he kept his peace. Antony's breakfast, which had been
sent to keep warm, came back at this point in a rather charred
condition, and he didn't eat much of it. Which was unusual
for him, and enough to tell Jenny, who had returned by that
time, that something was in the wind. However, she raised no
objection when Antony phoned Lieutenant Hennessey and
made an appointment for eleven o'clock. She was given an
only slightly expurgated account of the talk with His Excellency, and merely said when her husband had finished, 'I
don't think it matters at all. Diplomatic immunity won't stop
bullets.'

Antony was still pondering this remark when he and Roger left for their engagement.

II

Lieutenant Hennessey's mood might have been expected to be less mellow this morning, but he seemed unaffectedly glad to see them. 'You've come to tell me that you've proof this protégé of yours is innocent,' he told them, almost jovially, but obviously prepared to disbelieve any evidence they might have to place before him. 'I'll be glad to listen to you, of course, but I may as well tell you before we start that our investigations have uncovered nothing in Tengrala Nema's favour.'

'Tell me frankly,' said Antony, seating himself, 'did you have us followed when we left you the other day?'

Hennessey chuckled. 'I think you know the answer to that, Mr Maitland.'

'I think so too, but I'm not out to make trouble.'

'I never thought so for a moment. I don't know where you acquired the facility, but I must suppose you're up to all the tricks in the book when it comes to shaking off a tail.'

'My misspent youth,' said Maitland solemnly. 'The exercise didn't have the desired outcome then?'

'No, and after what happened on Christmas morning – ' He broke off there, seeing Maitland's quick frown. 'An unpleasant thing, I agree with you there, but I hoped that after what happened – or rather, was intended to happen – you'd have agreed that your friend Tengrala Nema wasn't worth bothering about.'

'I'm afraid I didn't agree with you about that before, and I don't now. But it's not about his affairs that I've come to see

157

you, not directly at any rate. Though certainly what I have to say affects him in a way.'

'Are you trying to be deliberately mystifying, Mr Maitland?'

'Far from it. I want your help, and I'm now prepared to be frank with you on certain matters which before I felt bound to keep to myself.'

'I gather from the cautious wording of that statement that you still don't intend to be perfectly open with me.'

'No, Lieutenant, I'm afraid not. But you will listen to me?' he added with a certain eagerness in his tone.

'Oh, I'll listen. That's what I'm here for after all.'

'That and a few other things, I imagine,' said Roger, entering the conversation suddenly. 'But I've been with Mr Maitland all along in this and I may tell you now that I back up his conclusions absolutely.'

'Thank you, Mr Farrell. What are these conclusions?' Hennessey queried.

'Before I start I should tell you that we are neither of us now in any way connected with the Embassy.'

'Then young Nema's fate is no longer of any interest to you.'

'I didn't say that. It's of no interest to us as representatives of Her Majesty's Government, but as a matter of abstract justice it's of the very greatest concern.'

'Abstract justice being a thing you believe American law to be a little short in?'

'Nothing like that. All I think is that the police here are men like the rest of us, fallible like the rest of us, and as likely to be wrong as the police in my own country. Besides, in my opinion there was a deliberate attempt to frame Tengrala.'

'Nicely put, Mr Maitland. And now that's all clarified

158

between us, what's this story of yours?'

'I'll try to be brief. When I saw Tengrala Nema and formed my own conclusions as to his involvement, or lack of it, in the murder of Peter Ngala he confided in me the fact that, besides Mr Adams and his wife who had never actually visited the apartment, he had only six friends in New York, one of whom, a woman, had a set of keys.'

'To Tengrala Nema's apartment?'

'Exactly. To be precise, one key to the building and one to the door of the apartment itself. The other five had also visited him there. So you will see that the woman concerned, or anyone to whom she might have lent the keys, would have been in a position to go there in Tengrala's absence and extract the car keys and the rifle.'

'You'll forgive me for saying, Mr Maitland, that I find your explanation lacking in candour still.'

'You want to know why the rifles were there, and how intimate these friends I mentioned are. They were close enough friends, I understand, and regular visitors, but as for the rest I'm afraid I can't enlighten you.'

'Can't, Mr Maitland, or won't?'

'In the circumstances I think it's fair to say, can't. Do you want me to go on?'

'Certainly. Half a loaf, they say – '

'I hoped you might feel that way. You will admit at least, Lieutenant, that as there were other keys besides the ones that were in Tengrala's possession it is by no means a foregone conclusion that he is the guilty party.'

'There would certainly have been enquiries made among these people if he had been even as open with us as you are being now, and particularly, of course, of the woman. Is that what you hope will happen?'

159

'Things have become a little more urgent than that. The woman you see – '

'I take it you're implying that she visited young Nema because there was an affair between them?'

'Yes, both he, and she when I saw her, didn't attempt to deny that. And this in spite of the fact that she was living under the protection of another man. I think the liaison with Tengrala was entered into solely for the purpose of getting the keys.'

'You're entitled to your opinion, of course. Is that what you believe too, Mr Farrell?'

'It is,' said Roger. It sounded true enough, and Antony couldn't help wondering at what point his friend had come round so whole-heartedly to his own point of view.

'Then I think it's time you told me her name.'

'That's the whole purpose of my visit. Her name is – I should say was – Margaret Charron.'

Just for a moment Hennessey sat and stared at him. 'Charron?' he said. 'The woman who was murdered in the Village yesterday?'

'Precisely. Although it didn't occur in your precinct I had hoped you would have heard of the matter.'

'Certainly I have. I have also heard that there was no mystery about it. This man she was living with – '

'Joel Harte.'

' – was caught practically red-handed. And what you tell me, Mr Maitland,' he added with satisfaction, 'supplies the motive well enough.'

'That was not my intention. When we saw Mr Harte on Christmas Eve it was quite obvious that he had no idea that Margaret Charron had been dividing her favours between him and another man.'

'She wasn't killed until yesterday, late afternoon I understand. What you probably call tea-time, Mr Maitland. There was plenty of time for him to have found out in the meantime.'

'He didn't learn it from us. And do you think it was the kind of thing she would be likely to have confided in him?'

'No, I suppose not. Are you going to tell me that the motive was not jealousy, but because she was his accomplice in the murder of Peter Ngala, and perhaps he feared her discretion?'

'You're going too quickly, Lieutenant. I wasn't going to tell you anything of the kind. You're forgetting the other four people who were close friends of Tengrala's.'

'And what have they to do with it?'

'I'll give you their names if you like.' He did so, and Hennessey wrote them down carefully, though he added, looking up when he had finished,

'I'm not at all sure that exercise was worth the doing, Mr Maitland.'

'It was, and I hope you'll come to agree with me. They all share an apartment, rather a seedy apartment, also in Greenwich Village, which seems to be rented under Miss Crashaw's name. I should add that she and Jean le Bovier are living together, not just under the same roof, but in the usual sense in which that phrase is used.'

'The Frenchman? That's a strange household, isn't it?' Hennessey looked down at his list of names. 'A Frenchman, an Irishman, and a German.'

'I believe the three men had some previous acquaintance. Noella Crashaw ... well, she's very much in love with le Bovier, but I don't believe he returns her affections.'

'Are you trying to tell me that one of these three men,

rather than Joel Harte, may have killed Margaret Charron? If that's so, you should be talking to my opposite number who's in charge of the investigation, not to me.'

'I *am* trying to tell you that, and the matter *does* concern you, Lieutenant. I think Margaret Charron's keys to Tengrala's apartment were used when the rifle and the car keys were removed and replaced. I don't think that was at Joel Harte's instigation.'

'Whose then?'

'That of Jean le Bovier. I think that when Peter Ngala was killed Miss Charron drove the car and he used the rifle. I think too that they were lovers, and that when he discovered that her task of getting the key from Tengrala had been accomplished by becoming intimate with him he was so frantic with jealousy that he killed her.'

'There's an argument against that last statement, Mr Maitland. Apparently he had condoned her living with Harte.'

'Yes, and perhaps that was only because he himself was involved with Miss Crashaw. But the real point, I'm afraid, is that Tengrala is not a white man. He referred to him – not knowing that I understood his own language – as *moricaud*. That might roughly be translated as blackamoor, in any case it's a rather derogatory term.'

'That's all very well, but a man can dislike Blacks without having cause for jealousy. And even granted that you're right, what is this le Bovier's motive supposed to be for killing Peter Ngala? And even more to the point, why should the woman have helped him?'

'I have my own ideas about that. I can't explain them to you without betraying a confidence. I think, however, that if an investigation were to be started – '

'I don't suppose you realise it, Mr Maitland,' said Hennessey, shaking his head at him in an admonitory way, 'but you're asking me to make a fool of myself in front of my colleagues. Have you any other proof to offer?'

'Of the six, they were the only two to express belief in Tengrala's guilt. The others were all quite sure that it was a thing he couldn't have done.'

'Proof, Mr Maitland?' asked Hennessey quizzically.

'You don't need to remind me it's very far from that. I might add that neither of them showed any horror at an act of terrorism such as shooting Peter Ngala, but you'll tell me that isn't proof either.'

'I'm very much afraid ... I appreciate that you're sincere about that, Mr Maitland, and believe this rather far-fetched story you've told me, but unless you can give me something definite – '

'I know, you'll do nothing. Don't think I'm blaming you, Lieutenant, I didn't have much hope when I came here. Only I'm not equipped to undertake the kind of investigation that's required, particularly in a country where I have no standing except as a visitor. I had hoped that you would take the matter at least a few steps further.'

'I'm sorry, that's quite impossible.' Hennessey's tone was definite. 'If you could see your way to confide in me a little further – '

'I'm sorry too, but that's also out of the question. I have to thank you for your courtesy, Lieutenant,' said Antony, rising. 'I do see your point of view, and you've been very patient with us.'

Hennessey might speak firmly, but there was still a little uncertainty in his manner. 'Are you going to take this story of yours to the man in charge of the investigation?' he asked.

163

'I warn you, Mr Maitland, he may not be as patient with you as I have been.'

'No, I shan't do that. If you won't listen I realise there's no hope of getting anyone to.'

'What do you propose to do then?'

'If I said, wait and see, you might accuse me of taking the matter too lightly. But before we go there is one thing, Lieutenant – '

'What's that?' Friendliness and suspicion were blended in Hennessey's tone.

'How was this wretched girl killed? If you know how, that is.'

'Hit over the head with a knick-knack of some kind, I didn't trouble to remember the details.'

'But you said Joel Harte was caught practically red-handed?'

'Someone had called the police and asked them to investigate a disturbance in their apartment. Two of them arrived to find the door open and Harte inside with the weapon in his hand. He said, of course, that he had only just come in and picked it up without thinking, but we've all heard that one before.'

'Thank you, Lieutenant. That's really all and we'll leave you in peace now,' said Antony, getting up and making for the door. 'I'm sorry you wouldn't listen but I'd have been even more surprised if you had.'

He was gone, and Roger after him, before Hennessey could respond, and the Lieutenant found himself muttering, 'I hope you enjoy the rest of your stay,' to the empty air. But he was looking mystified as he sat down again slowly, and after about five minutes' cogitation he pulled the telephone towards him.

Jenny was alone when they got back to the hotel. Meg had phoned, she said, to say that the rehearsal was likely to go on at least until six or seven o'clock. 'We'll have lunch up here,' said Roger decisively, and when Antony went to the telephone to find out what was available he could hear his friend regaling Jenny with an account of their talk with Lieutenant Hennessey. 'The chap was amiability itself,' he concluded, 'but it was no use, he wouldn't buy it.'

Knowing the others' tastes well enough Maitland ordered without consulting them, and then turned back to the room almost prepared to be angry. But he had learned painfully over the years that there was nothing Jenny disliked so much as being kept in the dark about what was going on, particularly if there was likely to be danger, and this, he realised, was Roger's way of reminding him of the fact. 'So there's nothing for it, love,' he said as lightly as he could, 'but to take the matter into our own hands.'

'But how can you do that? I know what you think, but – '

'By going to see the four remaining conspirators, if possible all together,' said Antony.

'But they must be . . . Antony, the kind of men they are they must be dangerous. Even if they're not armed,' she added.

'Yes, I think they are. Dangerous, I mean. In a way, Jenny, that's what I'm relying on.'

'That doesn't make sense,' she protested.

'Perhaps you're right. You have to remember, love, I've got one fairly useful weapon myself.'

'You haven't – '

'He means he can talk the hind leg off a donkey,' said Roger. Antony had been conscious for some time that his friend's spirits were rising at the prospect of action, while he himself was only coldly aware of the difficulties ahead. There was, too, the undoubted fact that Jenny had lost her serene look, and the further fact that she would never try to hold him back only made matters worse. 'There's just a chance that we can do some good,' he assured her, 'so I feel we've got to try. After all, Joel Harte has his point of view and so has Tengrala.'

'Not to mention Sir Huntley,' said Jenny a little dryly.

'Yes, but I'll be honest with you, love, the diplomatic angle isn't my main concern.'

'One of your damned crusades,' said Jenny quoting.

'Yes, I suppose that's fair enough. I'm also angry, but that's beside the point. We can but try, and if it doesn't come off there's no harm done.'

Except that you'll worry about it for the rest of your life, thought Jenny, but she was wise enough not to say it aloud. She also wondered whether, without Roger's intervention, Antony would have been so frank with her, but that was another thought she kept to herself. 'I can't see why you should want to get them all together,' she said.

'Because . . . I shall have to play it by ear, love, it's no good trying to explain to you now.' But at that moment, to his relief, a knock on the door heralded their meal.

Jenny was rather silent while they ate, and Roger was only too obviously keeping his effervescent spirits in check in deference to his friend's mood. As they went downstairs later to look for a cab he said, rather defensively, 'It really was the best thing, you know.'

Maitland didn't pretend to misunderstand him. 'I nearly lost my temper all over again,' he confessed, 'but Jenny's happier . . . well, happy is hardly the word but a little less apprehensive, when she knows what's going on. So I'm glad you forced my hand.'

'We're taking a chance, not phoning ahead,' said Roger, harking back to a point about which there had already been some argument.

'Not so much of a chance as if we *had* phoned,' Antony retorted. 'We'd probably have found them scattered to the ends of the earth by the time we got there.' And that was true, but it would be the merest chance, he realised, if the four people he wanted to see were all together just at that time. And if he had been truthful with himself he would have admitted that an excuse to postpone, or perhaps give up altogether the confrontation he was seeking would not have been unwelcome.

IV

Afterwards he thought that if his feelings had not been so mixed things would never have gone as they did. The natural perversity of events would have delayed a course of action that called for the presence of four people besides himself and Roger. Each of the four had his own life to live. But luck favoured them. That was how Roger put it later and Antony didn't contradict him. Again they went up through the shabby house, and again Noella Crashaw opened the door to them. 'Have you come again about Tengrala?' she asked.

'Indirectly,' said Maitland, and as promptly as if the word had summoned a genie from a bottle Jean le Bovier appeared at the girl's shoulder.

'I think,' he said, 'we've had enough of your questions.'

'I'm sorry you feel that way. Are your two friends with you?'

167

'Michael and Friedrich? Yes, they are here.' The Frenchman looked wary.

'Then I should very much like a few words with all of you
together. I promise it won't take long.'

'Oh, let the man in,' said O'Shaughnessy's voice. 'We're
not getting anywhere with our discussion, perhaps he can
throw some fresh light on it.'

Le Bovier backed away, though unwillingly. Antony and
Roger went into the little room, which somehow Michael
O'Shaughnessy's expansive presence seemed to make intoler-
ably overcrowded. Noella shut the door behind them and
when le Bovier had seated himself, perched herself on the arm
of his chair.

'Sit down, sit down the both of you,' said O'Shaughnessy,
who seemed to have constituted himself spokesman for the
moment. Schiller, as seemed to be customary with him, was
silent. It was impossible to tell whether he was glad or sorry
for the interruption.

'What were you discussing?' asked Roger curiously. Left to
himself Maitland would probably not have asked that, feeling it unlikely that he would get a truthful answer, but
O'Shaughnessy replied without hesitation.

'You know so much of our affairs, you'll appreciate the
present situation is a rather complicated one. Should we go
or stay?'

'The question is, where would you go?'

'To Bosegwane, where else? Fred and I have a feeling that
would be leaving Tengrala in the lurch, not to mention our
other friend, Joel.'

'I do not trust that one,' said Jean flatly.

'But what good would it do him to betray us?' said Schiller,
coming to life unexpectedly. 'His best chance is that the sen-

tence would be lenient because he has committed a crime of passion, which you, Jean, should understand.'

'Why me particularly?' le Bovier asked quickly, and the question sounded angry.

'In France it has long been the custom – '

'Yes, I see. All the same – '

'I appeal to you, Mr Maitland.' That was Schiller again. 'Would it help him to admit that Margaret was part of a conspiracy – I use your own word – to foster revolution in an African country, and that he knew what she was doing, even though he proposed to take no active part?'

'No, I don't think it would help him. But I'm glad you brought up the subject. It's Margaret Charron's death I want to talk to you about.'

'You said – ' began Noella accusingly.

'I said, Miss Crashaw, that our visit dealt with Tengrala's affairs indirectly. I don't agree, you see, that the death of Peter Ngala and the death of Margaret Charron are two completely unrelated events.'

'But that's ridiculous,' le Bovier began, and was interrupted without ceremony by Michael O'Shaughnessy.

'Are you telling us Joel killed Ngala too?'

'I don't think he killed anybody.'

'Then are you accusing Tengrala?'

'No.' He let that sink in for a moment, and then added deliberately, 'I think you, Monsieur le Bovier, killed them both.'

That brought Noella Crashaw to her feet, her hands curled until they looked suspiciously like claws. 'That's a wicked thing to say,' she said in a shaken voice. Le Bovier put up a hand and pulled her down against his shoulder.

'I will deal with it, *ma mie*. I'm not altogether familiar with

169

legal terms, Mr Maitland, but would not such a remark constitute either libel or slander?'

'Slander certainly,' said Antony cheerfully, 'but the defence of truth is a good one at law. At least it is in England, and I don't suppose it's so very different here.'

'But where there is no truth ... are you not afraid I shall take some action?'

'Mr O'Shaughnessy said just now that we knew, my friend and I, a good deal of your circumstances. You've put yourselves outside the law, I don't think you can turn round now and ask for its protection.'

'I thought that sooner or later the threats would come,' said le Bovier, with a pretty good attempt at a sneer. 'You're telling us we must listen to your lies, otherwise you'll make our position untenable with the authorities.'

'We do think there might be some questions asked about the rifles in Tengrala's apartment,' said Antony thoughtfully. 'And about any consignments that preceded them as well.'

O'Shaughnessy gave a sudden shout of laughter. 'He's right, Jean,' he said. 'Not that I believe for a moment ... but at least we'll have to listen.'

'Do you agree, Friedrich?' asked le Bovier.

'It seems we have no choice.'

Jean possessed himself of Noella's hand. 'Very well,' he said. 'We will listen, *chérie*, and you will not worry.'

'If you say I needn't, Jean, but I don't like it,' she assured him.

'I'm afraid, Miss Crashaw, you will like it still less in a moment,' Maitland told her. 'My first question is for you, you see.'

'I thought you knew it all,' sneered le Bovier.

'I think I do.' That was said with confidence, and probably

only Roger realised the uncertainty that lay behind the words. 'But I should like, you see, to convince these friends of yours ... haven't you ever wondered, Miss Crashaw, what exactly Monsieur le Bovier's relationship with Margaret Charron was?'

'We were all friends. Miss Charron was living with Mr Harte.'

'Yes. Do you know if they had considered the possibility of marriage?'

'They both regarded it as a permanent relationship,' she assured him.

'You know now that Miss Charron was in possession of the key to Tengrala Nema's apartment, and that they were lovers.' He was watching le Bovier's hands as he spoke, and saw them clench at his words.

'Tengrala may not have told you the truth.'

'Now I thought you were a partisan of his, Miss Crashaw.'

'I don't think he would commit a murder, but everyone tells lies sometimes.'

'So they do. But in this case, you know, Miss Charron admitted the fact to me. I don't think she would have done so if it hadn't been true, do you?'

'No ... no, I don't think even Margaret – '

'And where there are two lovers there may well be more. At least one more,' he added, and let his eyes stray to the man at her side.

'I suppose so, but not Jean.'

'That's enough!' said le Bovier. 'These insinuations – ' He began to get up.

'I think we'll be after hearing what else he has to say,' said O'Shaughnessy. He did not move, but his manner was commanding and Jean sank back in his chair again.

'Thank you, Mr O'Shaughnessy.' Maitland's tone had taken on a little dryness. 'Perhaps you've asked yourself sometimes, Miss Crashaw, where Monsieur le Bovier is when he goes out without you?'

'We each live our own lives.' For the first time there was a little uncertainty in her voice.

'*Man's love is of man's life a thing apart, 'tis woman's whole existence.* Have you ever heard that rather trite saying, Miss Crashaw?'

'I don't know what you mean.'

'That I think if you're honest with yourself you'll admit that much of the devotion has been on your side, and not on his.'

'No, no! It just isn't true.'

'You may remember that the last time Mr Farrell and I came here we had quite a long conversation with Monsieur le Bovier alone.'

'Yes, of course I remember.'

'In the course of that conversation we told him, as we had told you previously, of Margaret Charron's liaison with Tengrala Nema. You may believe me when I tell you that the knowledge was distasteful to him. Has he ever shown any sign of discriminating against Tengrala because of his colour?'

'No, of course not.'

'Nevertheless he spoke of him disparagingly in his own tongue, which I'm afraid he didn't realise that I understood. If you won't take my word for it, Miss Crashaw, you may ask Mr Farrell. He was present at the time.'

The girl came unsteadily to her feet, her eyes fixed beseechingly on Roger's face. 'Is it true?' she asked.

'It's perfectly true that Monsieur le Bovier first spoke very highly of Miss Charron, and then was much disturbed by what we had to tell him,' said Roger precisely.

'But that needn't necessarily mean ... Jean, you told me often when you went out that it was business and I needn't worry my head about it. Was that where you were? With her?'

Suddenly le Bovier was on his feet, shaking off the hands that clasped his arm. '*Allez-vous faire pendre ailleurs,*' he spat at her viciously. And then to Maitland, no less vehemently, '*Balourd!*'

'*Au contraire,*' said Maitland lightly. 'I think I got the result I was aiming for, don't you?' He took his eyes from his adversary for a moment and looked at Noella Crashaw, adding more gently, 'In case you're in any doubt about it, my dear, I'm afraid your Jean is not particularly pleased with either of us.'

She glanced for a moment from Maitland to Roger and then collapsed in a heap in the chair le Bovier had just vacated and began to cry. 'But that still doesn't mean,' she said through her sobs, 'that he killed her.'

'It means no more than that he had as good a motive as Joel Harte for doing so.'

'I haven't admitted – ' le Bovier began.

'There's more to come. I'm sorry to distress you, Miss Crashaw. Would you like to go into the other room?'

'No, no, I want to hear.'

'And so do we,' said O'Shaughnessy, still with that air of command. 'That goes for you too, doesn't it, Fred?'

'Indeed it does,' Schiller agreed. 'Though what has passed already is no more than I suspected.'

Michael gave him a hard look, before turning again to Maitland. 'You told us, if I remember,' said Michael, 'that there was a connection between the two murders. I should like to know how you make that out.'

'The main connection is that they were both committed by the same man.'

'According to you.'

'Yes, but I'm hoping to bring you round to my way of thinking. Do you mind answering a personal question, Mr O'Shaughnessy? I believe you were previously in the French Foreign Legion, and that Herr Schiller and Monsieur le Bovier were your companions in arms.'

'There's no secret about that.'

'No, but what I want to ask you may prove embarrassing. What was the motive behind your leaving, and seeking employment as mercenaries, in this case in the service of a man who'd like to overthrow the government of Bosegwane?'

'There's no secret about that either. Money, or the prospect of it.'

'Would you agree with that, Herr Schiller?'

For the first time in their acquaintance Friedrich Schiller smiled. 'It was certainly my motive,' he agreed.

'Don't listen to him,' said le Bovier suddenly. 'The fact that Margaret and I were lovers doesn't mean a thing.'

'Doesn't it? I think it means a good deal,' said Maitland. 'It means that when you wanted the key to Tengrala's apartment you trusted her to get it for you, though you didn't foresee the means she would use. And it also means, I think, that when you had the rifle safely in your possession she drove Tengrala's car for you while you shot Peter Ngala.'

'That isn't – ' But le Bovier broke off there, seeing Michael O'Shaughnessy coming slowly to his feet. 'Don't listen to him,' he said again.

'I'm listening,' said O'Shaughnessy, 'and I'm not believing anything ... yet. What I should like to know,' he added, turning to Antony, 'is what their motive could have been for such a thing. We agreed there was no reason that Tengrala should have done it, but I think the same applies to Jean.'

'You and Herr Schiller have both been very frank with me in telling me your reason for changing your employment. I wonder, Monsieur le Bovier, if you would be equally frank?'

'For the same reason.'

'Yes, I see, but I don't believe a word of it.' He turned a little to face O'Shaughnessy and Schiller. 'It may interest you to know some of the things that this dear friend of yours said at that first interview of ours, when we spoke of the conspiracy. Of Tengrala he said, *il perdu son temps*.'

'If I thought he was wasting his time, that is hardly incriminating,' Jean put in.

'No, but it does rather discount what you were saying about being in this thing for purely mercenary reasons. If the attempt was useless, how could you profit? I think, gentlemen, you must admit that Monsieur le Bovier was not altogether in sympathy with your aims.'

'What else did he have to say?' asked O'Shaughnessy.

'He referred to Herr Schiller as brainless, and to you, Mr O'Shaughnessy, as being wrong-headed. Or was it the other way round? I think that's approximately what you meant, isn't it, Monsieur le Bovier?'

'I won't stay here and listen to this.'

'Oh, yes, you will.' O'Shaughnessy moved quickly for so big a man, and took up his stance with his back against the door. 'But you've yet to explain to us, Mr Maitland, why he should have done these things of which you accuse him?'

'In the case of Miss Charron I think it was jealousy, pure and simple, if those words can ever be applied to so unpleasant a failing. I might add that we heard him make an appointment with her, before we left here the day she died. At least, he was speaking to a woman, whom he addressed as *chérie* and cautioned to mind what she said. Margaret Charron, I think, helped him because she loved him, and because there was nothing in Communism that went against her preconceived ideas.'

'Communism?' The word was no more than a growl.

'What is your purpose in trying to engineer this coup in Bosegwane, Mr O'Shaughnessy?'

'Certainly not that. There's the mercenary side, I admitted that to you, but this man who calls himself "King" is no friend to the west, I think nothing but good can come of his removal.'

'And you, Herr Schiller?'

'I agree with my friend.'

'Well, I can't pretend that Monsieur le Bovier was at all open with me, but I must tell you that I gained the distinct impression, from things he said when he was shaken by the realisation of Margaret Charron's infidelity, that his sympathies lay with the Soviets. And I think you don't realise it, gentlemen, but Peter Ngala's murder might have been a definite gain to them.'

'How?'

'Because if it could be proved, or even strongly suggested, that it had been done by the son of Bosegwane's ambassador to the United Nations, it would have given the president of Timkounou, who is Peter Ngala's father, an excuse to invade Bosegwane. And that in turn would give the USSR an excuse to intervene in the matter without coming up against world opinion. It would also have put paid to the coup you planned and your further prospects of gainful employment. That, I think, is the motive for Peter Ngala's death and the very

176

definite attempt that was made to incriminate Tengrala. You may decide for yourselves – '

He had no need to finish, even as he was speaking Michael O'Shaughnessy had moved, again with surprising quickness. Before anyone could stop him he had le Bovier by the throat and was shaking him as a terrier might shake a rat. 'All right then, Jean, my boy,' he said, 'let's have the truth of it. You've been playing false with Noella here, were you cheating us too?'

V

'But I don't understand,' said Jenny, much later that evening. Again they were dining upstairs, this time in the Farrells' room at Roger's suggestion. He knew well enough that neither Meg nor Jenny would be satisfied until they had heard the whole story, and though Antony would have been glad enough to keep silent on the matter at least for that evening, one look at Jenny's face when they got back to the hotel was enough to convince him that something more in the way of reassurance was needed than the mere fact that they were both physically safe. So he had started his story, prompted on occasion by Roger, and even Meg had listened in silence. But at the point when Michael O'Shaughnessy took matters into his own hands Jenny could contain her questions no longer. 'You may have convinced, or half-convinced, the other three conspirators that le Bovier had committed two murders, but where did you go from there?'

'I didn't need to go anywhere,' said Antony, rather smugly. 'O'Shaughnessy had the matter very well in hand. He's a big man, I told you that, and a very formidable one when he gets angry. And there's no doubt about it at that point he was very angry indeed.'

'Did he kill le Bovier?' asked Meg brightly.

'No, thank goodness, that would have taken some explaining. He seemed to mean to throttle him at first, but then I think he realised that there was no chance of Jean talking with a pair of hands round his throat.'

'May I ask you something, darling?' said Meg. 'Had you worked things up deliberately to that point?'

'Let's just say I was relieved at the outcome,' said Antony, with a rather apologetic look in Jenny's direction.

'You're giving them the impression all this took place in a vacuum,' said Roger. 'A good deal was going on at the same time. Noella Crashaw, for instance, flung herself on O'Shaughnessy and seemed to be trying to scratch his eyes out. She's about half his size or less, but still I dare say he might have found it inconvenient if Schiller hadn't taken a hand too. He just went up behind Noella and took her in a kind of bear's hug and held her like that until she collapsed into a sort of hysterical sobbing. At that point he laid her on the sofa and seemed to forget all about her, coming back and standing watching his two comrades quite dispassionately.'

'Yes, he's not a chap who's easily rattled,' said Antony. 'If it had seemed that murder was about to be committed, Roger and I would have had to do something about it, or try to, but as it was O'Shaughnessy changed his tactics, loosened his grip on le Bovier's throat a little, and started banging his head against the wall instead. Le Bovier's head I mean, not his own.'

'But – ' Jenny began to protest.

'No, love, I can't have you wasting your sympathy on a man like that,' said Maitland firmly. 'It was by far the best thing that could have happened.'

'I don't see that he'd be able to talk any better that way than when he was being strangled,' said Jenny rather severely.

'No, but it didn't go on for very long. And – this did surprise me Roger, didn't it you? – it got results. He blurted out the whole story, his detestation of capitalism, his recruitment by Communist agents, and the difficulty he had always had in keeping his real feelings to himself. When the plot was hatched against Tengrala, intended to produce exactly the result Sir Huntley feared, he had used Margaret Charron to get the keys of the apartment because he could see that Tengrala was attracted to her, but he never dreamed until we told him how far she'd gone to get them. At that point I suggested to O'Shaughnessy that it might be a good idea to get the whole thing down in writing, and after a little further persuasion le Bovier agreed.'

'What sort of persuasion?' asked Meg suspiciously.

'Nothing very drastic,' said Antony hurriedly with a glance in Jenny's direction. 'You'll have gathered by now that le Bovier is a weak man morally. All this took some time, of course, but when the statement was finished I called the police, and at my suggestion they routed out Lieutenant Hennessey to come with the people from the local precinct.' He paused and sighed. 'We've been explaining ever since.'

'But I still don't understand,' Jenny protested. 'Sir Huntley ... and then all these people will get into trouble, won't they? Tengrala and the others?'

'Nothing has been said about the plot to overthrow the government of Bosegwane,' said Antony. 'Le Bovier's confession cites merely the desire to foment trouble as his reason for killing Peter Ngala. The police are only too glad to leave Roger and me out of it, so nothing will ever be known of the concern Her Majesty's Government felt about all this, and the State Department too, if I understood H.E. correctly. For the moment I think le Bovier is convinced that it will be best to leave the secondary conspiracy, the one he was pretending to be part of, out of the story, though I agree he may change his mind about that at any time.'

'Well then – ' said Meg.

'At the moment O'Shaughnessy and Schiller are merely visitors to this country, free to leave at any time. When we were alone again I advised them to do so immediately, before their passports could be impounded and they could be held as material witnesses or whatever it is they do over here.'

'What about Tengrala?'

'The police have his passport, but I had a talk with Hennessey about that after the local chaps had gone. There are no flies on him, I can tell you that, he's perfectly aware that the presence of the rifles in the apartment means that our friend was up to something of which the authorities wouldn't approve, but in the circumstances he says there will be no difficulty about returning it to him. An easy way out of an awkward situation really.'

'That poor little girl, Noella something?'

'O'Shaughnessy told me she had an aunt or something living here in Manhattan. He'd take her round there before leaving. I'm afraid she's in for a bad time, but that's better surely than having two innocent men convicted of murder.'

'If all the witnesses have gone, won't the police need your evidence and Roger's?' asked Meg.

'They have their confession, that should be enough to get Joel Harte released, and Tengrala off the hook too. Quite frankly I don't care what happens after that.'

'The police may,' Meg pointed out. 'What if they want you

to stay here till the trial, it may be years and years if all I read about America is true.'

'That, I think, is where Sir Huntley comes in, and his contacts at the State Department.'

'But he's not very pleased with you,' said Jenny.

'I think you'll find everything has been forgiven and forgotten, or will be when he hears the whole story.'

'Well, if you say so,' said Jenny doubtfully.

'I do say so. I'm damned if I'm going to ring him at this time of night, for one thing it would probably annoy him, and for another I'll have to choose my words carefully with all this blasted diplomatic secrecy about.'

'You won't have to go to Washington again?'

'If I do we'll go together, love; but no, I don't think it will be necessary.'

And for once in his life when he ventured into the realms of prophecy it turned out that he was right.

Friday, 28th December

I

At first, however, it seemed that perhaps the decision not to ring the ambassador until the morning had been the wrong one. Sir Huntley sounded decidedly grumpy when Maitland finally got through to him. 'Now what do you want?' he enquired disagreeably.

'To tell you that the matter we spoke of has been cleared up, and I hope you will think satisfactorily.'

'Satisfactorily? Since you categorically refused to follow the guidelines I set down for you – '

'I wonder, Your Excellency, if you'd listen to me for a moment.'

'Have you really got anything to say?'

'A good deal, as a matter of fact.'

'Then you'd better come here.'

'No, sir, I don't think so. If you'd let me tell you … I'm getting used to this diplomatic double talk,' said Antony, 'and I think I can give you a pretty good picture of what's happened without compromising the situation in any way.'

'You don't think much of diplomats, eh?' For some reason Sir Huntley seemed to find the idea a cheering one. 'Well, if you get right down to it I don't think much of lawyers either.'

'No, Your Excellency. But you did ask my help,' Antony ventured.

'So I did, so I did. Well, you'd better tell me.'

After their previous conversation, this one was comparatively easy to put into words that the ambassador would understand but that wouldn't mean much to an outsider. 'So it amounts to this,' said Sir Huntley when the recital had finished, 'the New York Police Department have a confession from the murderer of Peter Ngala, citing as his motive a plot of Soviet origin to create bad blood between Timkounou and Bosegwane. The murder of this woman doesn't concern us but I suppose you consider having that cleared up equally a triumph.'

'As a matter of fact, sir, I do.'

'And the police knew nothing of this other matter?' Which Antony took to be a reference to Tengrala Nema's conspiracy.

'Nothing at all, though as it's possible le Bovier may enlighten them later I've taken the liberty of advising the other two men who were present last night to leave the country immediately. I shall also see the person about whom you were concerned in the beginning, and advise him to take the same steps.'

'Well, well, Antony, you seem to have thought of everything.'

Encouraged by this sudden friendliness Maitland was emboldened to make his plea. 'I think perhaps, Your Excellency, if any question arises of evidence being required from Roger Farrell and myself – '

'I've spoken to you before about all this formality. There's no need to worry about that, my boy. That can all be arranged. An affidavit – ' said Sir Huntley Gorsford vaguely. 'My friends in the State Department will be as pleased as I am at so satisfactory an outcome.'

'Then there's nothing more to worry about,' said Maitland, 'except – ' He hesitated.

'Except what?' asked His Excellency, still in the same friendly way.

'That business of the bombs, sir. Would you mind calling Uncle Nick and telling him about it. I mean, it's quite likely the papers at home will pick it up sooner or later, and I shouldn't like him and Vera to hear of it that way. He may believe you if you assure him that there's no further danger.'

'With all the pleasure in the world. You may be assured too, Antony, that I shall make sure this good work of yours is known in the proper quarters.' But Maitland, having gained what he wanted, was no longer listening very closely. His attention was only jerked back to the conversation when Sir Huntley enquired delicately, 'Do you think the principal of this young protégé of ours is in a position now to act?'

'I have a feeling that he is,' said Antony. 'But it's only a feeling, I don't think you should rely on it.'

'Well, well, we must hope for the best,' said Sir Huntley. 'I'll get on to Nicholas as you suggest, don't worry any more about that.'

He rang off without very much more ado, leaving Maitland to rejoin Jenny and Roger, who were waiting anxiously for the result of this conversation. 'I shall never, never, never understand the diplomatic mind,' he said.

II

He went after lunch to see Tengrala Nema, but found to his

185

relief the story did not need to be told over again. 'Michael and Friedrich spent the night here,' said Tengrala, 'having booked on a plane out of New York early this morning. They have told me all that happened, but I find it difficult to believe that Jean would have done such evil things.'

'I'm afraid you'll have to accept that he deliberately tried to implicate you for his own ends. In the circumstances I shouldn't feel too sorry for him if I were you. But what I wanted to tell you, Tengrala, was that Lieutenant Hennessey has promised to return your passport almost immediately. I think you should follow your friends' example when he does.'

'Yes, I see. You think that Jean may talk of our plans?'

'I think it possible, no more than that.'

'That is very bad,' said Tengrala seriously.

'Not too bad if none of you are here for the police to question,' said Antony. 'I don't think in those circumstances you'd find they had very much interest in the matter. But you might tell me one thing if you would. You said when I saw you before that you trusted me.'

'Yes, indeed I do.'

'Then how much difference will all this make to your plans?'

'None at all, I think. Everything is ready, and Michael has told me that he will advise immediate action, in case the story should leak out.'

'I see. Have you thought this out, Tengrala? What then will happen to your father?'

'I have told you, he is King Mbongo's man.' But Antony thought he detected a trace of uncertainty in the previously confident tones.

'Yes, and presumably he will be here when your plans take shape. If they're successful – '

'They will be successful.'

'*If* they are,' Antony repeated, 'what of him?'

'If he were in Bosegwane at the time of the uprising there would be executions, his among them.'

'You don't like the idea, do you?'

'I don't know how you understand that, but I have, I suppose, some filial feelings still.'

'Enough to see that vengeance, as you regard it, doesn't follow him here?'

'That will not happen,' said Tengrala positively. 'I have . . . I have been promised that. But if he should return – '

'Can you think of no action you could take to ensure that he doesn't?'

'No, I can't. Can you advise me, Mr Maitland?'

'I think perhaps I can. Your friend Mr Adams, you trust him too, don't you?'

'Yes, I do.'

'Then if you left a letter with him for your father, not to be forwarded to him before a certain date . . . I take it you could make a pretty good guess when the rising will take place?'

'Yes, I think so.'

'In that case it's very simple. Assure your father again of your sincerity in the action you've taken, and plead with him to seek political asylum in this country. I have always found the Americans a generous people,' he went on, and thought as he spoke that this was an echo of a conversation he had had with Meg and Roger when first he arrived. 'I'm sure such asylum would be granted, perhaps in time you could come back and make your peace with him.'

'He's a stubborn man, Mr Maitland, but perhaps when he sees how much better things will be . . . I do not know. But I should like to help him. I'll do as you say.'

'All right, Tengrala, then it only remains to say goodbye to you,' said Maitland, feeling all at once very far from home, very far out of his depth, and filled with nostalgia for the familiar shabbiness of chambers, for the courtrooms at the Old Bailey, and the fantastic façade of the Law Courts. But he cheered up again when he got back to the Hotel Majestic and saw that Jenny had again her serene look, and that she and Roger had been making a detailed plan for the rest of their stay.

'You're really very clever, Antony,' she said, 'to get things over so quickly. Now we can really enjoy our holiday.' But even as she spoke the telephone by the bed rang and Antony, being still on his feet, went across to answer it.

'It's Uncle Nick,' he said hollowly, with his hand over the mouthpiece. And as he spoke it occurred to him very forcibly that whatever Sir Huntley had been able to say by way of reassurance would only have gone to convince his uncle that a good deal had been happening of which he would not have approved. He lowered his hand and turned back to concentrate on the call and whatever denunciations Sir Nicholas might propose to hurl at him across the three thousand odd statute miles that Roger had mentioned.

Epilogue

Jenny was quite right, the rest of their holiday passed very pleasantly, though Meg was engaged with rehearsals right up to New Year's Eve when the dress rehearsal took place. She arrived home, tired but triumphant, no more than three minutes before midnight. Both Antony and Jenny were inclined to think she should be hurried straight to bed, but Roger, from long experience knew better. There had to be an unwinding period before there was any chance at all of her getting to sleep.

And on New Year's Day there was opening night. 'An Irishism in honour of our friend Mr O'Shaughnessy,' as Antony was quick to explain. They all attended that, though Antony at least had some qualms about doing so considering what had happened when the play was put on in England. Jenny was more concerned that the amount of unsolicited publicity would have prejudiced the critics against the performance, and whatever Roger thought about the matter he was keeping it to himself. But all was well, the audience proved appreciative, and the papers next morning held no terrors for them but only glowing praise. They could relax and enjoy themselves, but it was very noticeable that Antony had joined his friend in an eager perusal of the newspapers each morning, not to mention listening to the television news at night if they were home in time.

'Darling, what are you looking for so assiduously?' asked Meg one morning.

'Nothing in particular,' said Antony, hastily putting down the *New York Times*.

'But, darling – '

'You've been rather preoccupied, Meg, or you'd know the answer to that,' Roger told her. 'He wants the latest news from Bosegwane.'

'You never told me, did Tengrala get away all right?'

'He did,' said Maitland shortly. Then he relented. 'You see,' he said apologetically, 'I've never actually fomented a revolution before.'

'I wonder if Uncle Nick would agree with you,' said Jenny, smiling at him.

'I think so. Other types of mayhem, yes, but not revolution,' Antony insisted. 'And I must admit – '

'It's nothing whatever to do with you,' said Jenny and Meg in chorus.

Roger had been continuing his perusal of the paper. 'Well, you needn't wait any longer,' he said, looking up. 'King Mbongo has been deposed in a bloodless coup, and has taken refuge in Cauguera.'

'That's not a very good idea,' said Antony. 'They were part and parcel of the plot against him, weren't they?'

'I don't suppose he knows that. Anyway, I expect he'll end up in Libya or somewhere like that.' Roger had picked up his own paper again as he spoke. 'Here it is,' he said. 'Another chap with an unpronounceable name has taken over, who says democratic elections will be held and so on, all the usual stuff. And any of King Mbongo's supporters who wish to submit to the new regime will be made welcome. I hope none of them take that too seriously. President Joseph Ngala of Timkounou has sent congratulations, so that sounds as if he intended to make the best of the situation.'

'Bloodless, darling,' said Meg to Antony, in case the point had escaped him.

'You think that should comfort me?' He considered for a moment. 'Well, it does,' he admitted. 'I wonder how it came about that way though.'

'I expect,' said Jenny, 'it was because the supply of arms dried up. And Sir Huntley will be pleased,' she added.

'Much I care about that.'

'No, I know you don't, Antony, but just think. Even Uncle Nick won't be able to find anything more to grumble at, and that's something to be thankful for.'

Antony smiled at her. It was one of these occasions when, even with their closest friends, Roger and Meg, present, they might have been alone. 'My dearest love,' he said, 'you're right as usual. And as we're due home in about four days' time it's certainly a thought worth holding on to.'